FALSE SECURITY

Rogue Security and Investigation Series
Book Two

By Evan Grace

FALSE SECURITY

Crave Publishing, LLC
Kailua, HI 96734
http://www.cravepublishing.net/

Formatting: Crave Publishing, LLC

ISBN-13: 978-1-64034-381-8
ISBN-10: 1-64034-381-4

DEDICATION

To the survivors out there.

Author's Note:

The story is about a woman who survived domestic abuse. At times she thinks about things that have happened to her, and the abuse is shown—albeit brief it's still there. They may be triggers for some.

CHAPTER ONE

Shayla

When they call my name at the counter, I grab my coffee and make my way to one of the chairs in the corner. I take a sip and sigh happily as the hot liquid slides down my throat.

My coffeemaker broke this morning, but that wasn't the worst thing that happened. Our orange tabby, Lucifer—yeah, I know—threw up in my doorway, which I didn't know until I stepped in it. While I hobbled into the bathroom, Grant—or as I like to call him, Grunt—came running past me, hit the throw up, and went sliding across my hardwood floor.

He immediately started crying, quickly sliding into full meltdown mode. I grabbed him instead of cleaning my foot so I could stick him in the shower and clean him up. Once he was dried off, I wrapped him in a towel and sent him to his room to wait for me. I quickly rinsed my foot before cleaning up the floor in my room. If I didn't love that psychotic cat so much, I might've strangled him.

Once that was done, I headed into my son's room and leaned against the doorframe, watching him. He was sitting on his bed looking at one of his picture books. I walked over to join him on the bed, glanced at the book he was looking at, and smiled. *The Dog Man* series is his favorite. We love going to the library, and he'll go through each page. I read with him and work with him on his pronunciation. But sadness washed over me when I thought about everything that'd happened over the past two years.

My ex, Ryan, Grant's father, used to hit me...*badly*, and I stayed because I was scared to leave, and stupid. I'd been convinced that was the right thing to do; I had my child to think about, and he loved his daddy. Grant loved him all the way up until he walked in on his dad pinning me to the bed, hitting and biting me until I was covered in blood and bruises. Ryan had known our son was in the room, but he didn't stop because he knew it hurt me for our boy to see that. The next day, I went into the police station, pressed charges against him, and then filed for divorce. It was the last straw.

Grant was only three when it happened, and it was like someone had flipped a switch inside him. He became scared of men, never talking in front of them and taking a long time to relax in their presence.

We moved to Chicago last year, hoping that a change of scenery would do us both good, and it has, for the most part. My neighbor Luna watches him during the day while I work—she's a stay-at-home mom with three- and four-year-old girls. My sweet little Grunt does whatever they want, and they seem to love bossing him around.

He ran right up there when it was time to go. Grant always hugs Luna and then both girls, but he only waves and says, "Hi," to Luna's husband, Rocco. I hate that he's so skittish around men, even the good ones.

"Shayla?" I'm pulled from my thoughts by a woman's voice and look up to find my new friend Carrie coming toward me with her cute pregnant belly.

I smile. "Hi girlie, you look fantastic."

The beautiful blonde rubs her belly and smiles back. "Thanks." She sits down in the other chair. We met a few weeks ago, when there were no chairs free for her and I was on the love seat. I'd invited her to sit with me, and we ended up talking for a little while.

My son is my life, but it's nice to have adult conversation. I work for a temp agency, going where I'm needed but with the flexibility I sometimes require with a small child at home. Luckily in the divorce settlement I got alimony and child support, which leaves me comfortable enough right now that I can work part time if that's what Grant needs from me.

"Are you getting ready for the baby to come?" She's due any time now.

Carrie takes a sip of her tea. "We are. The nursery is ready, I'm doing cloth diapers, and I've got the service set up. My bag's packed, and I've got the baby's coming home outfit picked up."

"That's exciting." I haven't shared that I have a son, because then she'd find out about Ryan and the

3

mess that our relationship was. I'd rather keep that stuff private—it's easier that way.

"So I have a question, and a possible request." She looks hopeful. "Okay, first...I know you said you work for a temp agency, but I was wondering what type of work you do?"

"I do secretarial work, and when I lived in Madison, I was the manager of a law office." That's why I was able to nail Ryan to the wall when I filed for divorce. I could've stayed working there, but after my co-workers learned the truth about my home life, I just couldn't do it. I *had* to leave.

"That's perfect! Okay, so my husband and I work for a security and investigation company called Rogue. Well, I go on maternity leave soon, and our office manager is searching for my replacement. She's expecting as well, so we want someone who could step in and fill either role. This is just perfect that we met each other—it was like fate. You should come work for us."

"I'm not sure if I'm cut out for that right now," I tell her. "I just have some stuff that I'm dealing with."

"How about this: I'll email you, or Delilah will. We'll give you a rundown of the job, the hours, and the pay. If you decide you want it, we can talk more."

I give her my email and drink the rest of my coffee down. I'm ready to say goodbye to her, but she stays me with a hand on my arm. "I have one more thing. I know you're single, and I was wondering if you'd be opposed to being set up on a blind date."

"I don't know. I'm not really in a good place to date." What I *really* need is to have sex. Masturbating is all I've done since my divorce. It's less complicated than sharing my history with someone.

"Oh, *please*. I've got the perfect guy for you. His name's Erik, and he's *so* much fun. Don't take this the wrong way, but you seem like you could use some fun."

When *is* the last time I had fun? And I know Luna and Rocco would watch Grant, so…"If I do this, *I* will pick a place, and he can meet me. Deal?" That way if it's disastrous, I can make my escape. Shit, maybe I could get some decent sex out of it, and then I'd be good for another couple of years.

Carrie's smile widens like the Cheshire Cat's— she can tell my resolve is weakening. *Ugh.* "Sure, whatever makes you most comfortable," she chirps. "I'm sure he'll be fine with that. Plus, he's not available this weekend anyway, so we can shoot for next week, if you want? You'll have plenty time to think of a good spot."

Against my better judgment, I nod my head. "Ugh…Okay, set it up."

Right in the middle of the coffee shop, she starts squealing and clapping her hands.

I have a feeling saying "yes" was a mistake.

***

I take my time sheet over to the office manager and have her sign it for me. "Thanks for your help today, Shayla," she says.

"You're welcome. Just call the office if you need me again." I step out onto the sidewalk and start walking toward the bus stop. The doctor's office I was just at is one of the steady places I work—I come once a week to do some filing for them. I'd love to work there full time since they've got benefits and that would be better than Medicaid, which we have now. It's hard to find doctors who take new patients with the card.

Once I get home, I stop up at Luna and Rocco's apartment to get Grant. I knock, and the beautiful blonde opens the door, smiling at me. "Hi Shayla, how was work?"

"It was good, thanks. How was he today?"

Her smile only gets wider. "He was wonderful as always. We walked to the park and the library today. Grant really loved story hour, and Starr sat glued to his side while they listened. After we came back here, all three of them were exhausted, so they laid down on the floor in the living room and actually took a nap today."

"Great, thanks. Ummm…there was something I wanted to discuss with you. I've been offered a full-time job with amazing pay and benefits. It's to cover a woman's maternity leave, but they may keep me on after she gets back if it goes well, and I know it's a lot to ask—" Great, I'm babbling. I wasn't even going to consider it until I got the email from Delilah, the office manager.

Luna holds up her hand. "It's not a lot, and I'd love to watch him."

I heave a sigh of relief, because once most places hear he doesn't talk a lot, especially around men, they refuse to take him, assuming he's special needs. "Thank you so much."

She wraps her arms around me. "Don't thank me. We love you guys, and Shay, he's a good boy." Luna lets go of me and steps back. "When do you start?"

"It won't be for a couple of weeks, but I'll let you know as soon as I know for sure." Luna leads me into the living room where the kids are up now, watching *Moana*. My boy will watch anything the girls want, but that's just how he is. "Hey, my little Grunt!" He turns and his eyes light up.

"Mommy!"

On fast legs, he jumps up and races toward me. I wrap my arms around him, inhaling his sweet little boy scent. "Were you good today?"

He pulls back, smiling and nodding. His shaggy brown hair falls into his eyes. I brush it back. I should cut it—it's getting long, but I love it on him.

"Should we go home? Mom could use some snuggles. Wave bye to Luna, honey." My boy does one better and runs to her, hugging her quickly before running back to me. I turn back to Luna. "Oh, I was going to ask if you might be able to watch him all night next Saturday," I say. "I kind of told a friend she could set me up on a date."

Luna squeals and begins hopping up and down. "Yes, a hundred times *yes*! Oh my goodness, this is fantastic. Who is it?"

"I'm not sure. His name is Erik—that's all I know. I'm scared as hell, but I'll feel better about everything knowing Grant is safe here with you. I don't plan on staying out all night, but I didn't want to wake him up to take him home." He's spent the night here before when I've been too sick to take care of him. Luckily it hasn't happened a lot. I've returned the favor, watching their kids too.

"No worries, you just go out and have fun."

"Okay, we'll talk later. Bye, girls!" I call out to Starr and Lennon. Yes, Luna and Rocco are Beatles fans and named their daughters after members of the band. They're a totally bohemian and hippyish couple, and the best people I've ever met. I smile at the girls' distracted little goodbyes.

Lucifer greets us at the door when we come in. Grunt picks him up and carries him back to his bedroom, returning a few minutes later with one of his books tucked under his arm and Lucifer's front legs draped over it. His fat orange body is hanging there, but he's unperturbed because that's how much he loves Grant.

They lie side by side on the floor while Grant reads out loud to him. I head into my room, changing into shorts and a t-shirt. Then I head out to the kitchen to start dinner.

While we eat, I talk to him about my day, and he tells me about the park. Grant looks up at me and something about his eyes triggers a memory—my eyes burn as I remember that night. When I had seen my sweet little Grunt standing there in our bedroom, a part of me had died. His eyes had been wide with fear as Ryan hit me and bit me over and over, not stopping until he tired himself out.

Chills rack my body as I remember watching Ryan walk right by our son and ruffle his hair like he did all the time. I'd summoned up enough

8

strength to slide off the bed, wrap myself in the sheet, and crawl over to Grant. Bile burns my throat as I remember the way his body trembled as I held him to me. His tears slid silently down his face and I vowed right then and there that Ryan was *never* going to touch us again.

I get up from the table quickly. "Baby, Mommy's going to go to the bathroom quick." He doesn't look up from his plate.

After hurrying down the hall, knowing I only have seconds before scalding tears begin to spill down my face, I close the bathroom door and collapse onto the closed toilet seat. I bury my face in my towel to muffle the sound of my crying. Guilt is a heavy burden I bear, but how can I not? The first time Ryan hit me I should've ran—well, I ran the first time, but went back. I was weak and blinded by love.

I'll never let a man have any sort of power over me again. I'm not sure why I agreed to go on this blind date, but if he's good-looking and down, maybe I could just dust the cobwebs off my vagina and have sex. Because I *do* miss sex, and masturbation honestly gets super boring.

Once the tears dry up, I splash cold water on my face and then dry it off. I look in the mirror and luckily don't see any evidence of my breakdown. I take a deep breath and vow not to let the guilt drown me today.

CHAPTER TWO

Erik

The sounds of my breathing and my tennis shoes slapping the treadmill are all I hear as I finish up my morning jog. It's raining—otherwise, I'd be running in the park. There's usually an early morning yoga class, and the women are hot...and flexible. If the mood hit, I'd pick one up and go home with them for a little hardcore fucking. This weekend I won't be able to go out looking for a lady friend, though, because my fourteen-year-old sister is coming to stay with her favorite big brother.

Hell, at thirty, I'm technically old enough to be her *father*. My dad died when I was just a small boy—a carjacking gone wrong. The perp, a kid named Cesar, had been high as a kite and desperate and scared when he shot my dad. He'd only been fifteen when he went away, but my mom, being the saint she is, forgave him, counseled him, and got him on the right path. When he was released twenty years ago, my mom helped him start over.

Now he's married with a couple of kids and

serves as the assistant pastor at my step-dad, Tad's, church. Tad and my mom met when she was helping Cesar turn things around, and he got him his position. Tad and my mom married a year after they met and hadn't planned on having kids, but then Mom got pregnant with Gretchen.

Although lots of years separate us, we're extremely close. Gretchen may be a kid, but she's so fucking smart and funny, and I love spending time with her. She's not one of those irritating little shits…thank God.

I focus back on running, letting that runner's high hit me and flow through my body. It's rainy, hot, and humid as fuck today, but if the military taught me anything, it was how to focus and work through anything that may be a hurdle. It's been five years since I served in the Marine Corps, but all that shit stays ingrained in your brain. No matter what time I go to bed, I'm always up and running by five.

By the time I stop the treadmill and get off, I feel fucking soaked to the bone with sweat. I hurry home from the gym in the shitty weather, let myself in, and toss my keys, phone, and earbuds on my kitchen counter. In the living room, I jump up and on my pull-up bar, doing a set until my arms feel like jelly.

I finish with some crunches, and then some stretches before I down a protein shake and some eggs. After showering, I get dressed to go into work. I've been the head of surveillance at Rogue Security and Investigation for the past year, but I've worked there longer than that. The owner, Jack

Mackenzie, and I met through Egan, who's the IT specialist. Me and Jack hit it off and he hired me immediately. Next week a guy who served with him in the Army is starting. He'll be my counterpart.

If Jack trusts him, then so do I—this guy is supposed to be a good asset to our team, and if Jack says he'll fit, then he will. Some of the men helped the guy move into his place, but I'd been working on a case at the time. I head out to my Explorer and make the trek across town to the office.

Egan's very pregnant wife, Carrie, greets me from the front desk. "Looking beautiful as always, Carrie."

"You're such a charmer. Hey, I wanted to talk to you. Do you have a second?"

I lean against the counter and give her a flirtatious smile. "Are you finally leaving that husband of yours for me?"

"Haha, no, but I was wondering if I could set you up on a blind date. She's amazing, and *just* your type."

Carrie is the office matchmaker…or at least tries to be. "Big hair, big tits, and a small waist?" I ask.

She shakes her head and smiles. "You're terrible. She's perfect for you. I know Gretchen is coming to see you this week, so I told her maybe next week. Does that work?"

"Yeah, yeah, yeah, set it up." I hear her excited squeal while I head into the back, shaking my head. That girl is a nut.

"Oh, wait!" she calls out to me. I pause without turning around, my eyebrows raised. "She had only one *tiny* condition—she gets to pick the place, and

12

you'll meet her there. I'll let you know what she decides, okay?"

I roll my eyes and grunt as I continue walking. In my office, I pull up the case I just finished earlier in the week. I fill out my billable hours and put everything into an email that I send to our office manager, Delilah, so she can send out an invoice to the client.

Delilah is the only other woman that works here. She's Jack's daughter, and she's pregnant too. When I met her, she'd appeared really young and I thought he'd just given her the job because she's his kid. But it became obvious right away that *she's* the one who really runs things around here. She's respected by all the guys on our team.

By the time I'm ready to head home, I'm beat. I had two meetings with potential clients, and it's usually the same bullshit: following spouses that were possibly cheating or idiots stealing from their employers and not covering their tracks very well. Every now and then I'll help our bounty hunter track down a skip. I don't have a family waiting for me at home, so I can always leave town whenever I'm needed.

Don't get me wrong—I'm not lonely or unhappy with my life or the choices I've made. If I want female companionship for the night, I have no trouble finding a lady—or ladies—to oblige me. What can I say? I'm irresistible. The ladies love me…well, *and* the huge dick in my pants.

***

My sister carries the popcorn bowl into the living room and sits on one end of the couch while I sit on the other. She's been here since the day before, and we've already hit most of her favorites: The Cheesecake Factory (Lord help me), Navy Pier (Fuck my life), and her favorite candy store, Windy City Sweets. (At least the hot girl was working so *I* had some eye candy.)

We just got done eating a pizza and now we're watching a movie. "I'm going to have to increase my workouts as soon as you're gone," I mumble. "How can such a tiny little thing eat so much?" She looks a lot younger than she is; she's petite in stature, but all arms and legs.

I always used to call her "Tinkerbell." Her hair is a sort-of-rose-gold shade of blonde, and we've got the same blue eyes. That's where the similarities end, though. Like I said she's tiny, and I'm six-foot-six with muscles for days. Her skin is pale like porcelain, and my skin has a light olive tone to it.

It was in high school while playing football that I got the nickname "The Viking." I was the biggest and one of the fastest defensive linemen in our division. No one could get past me. I could've gone pro, but my senior year I met with a recruiter from the Marines, and that was all she wrote.

"What's this movie called again?" I ask as I settle deeper into the couch, grabbing a handful of popcorn.

"*My Girl*. I've never seen it, but Mom said it's amazing."

"I don't think I've ever heard of it." I signal to the remote with a nod of my head. "Let's get it started."

A while later, I look over at my sister, who's sobbing uncontrollably into her blanket. The little blond kid from *Home Alone* just died. It would've been nice if Mom warned Gretch, but *no*…now I'm dealing with an overly emotional teenager.

"I-I ca-can't be-believe he's dead!" Gretchen wails, and the next thing I know, she's curled up next to me, crying into my shirt.

I have to shut the movie off after the funeral scene because I can't hear what the fuck is happening. When Mom comes to get her tomorrow, we're having words. I swear the woman does this shit on purpose. She and my step-dad know my one true weakness is my baby sister. I'd do pretty much anything for her—even sitting through this cryfest she's having.

I can hear my bottle of Patrón calling my name from the kitchen, and right now I could drink the whole thing and be completely okay with it. It doesn't take long before Gretchen is passed out, curled up next to me. She's got a room here, so I carry her to bed. I grab my phone and my mom answers on the second ring.

"Hey, honey. How's it going?"

I sigh heavily into the phone. "Thank you *so* much for recommending *My Girl*. Your daughter bawled her eyes out, and then *passed out*—due to emotional exhaustion is my guess." My mom never buys the disgruntled act when it comes to Gretchen.

"Oh, stop. It's a great movie. She wanted to bring *Pitch Perfect*, but I knew you'd kill me if I let that happen." They all know about my aversion to any and every musical. I'll suffer through one if I have to, but I may bitch and moan the whole time.

I laugh into the phone. "Probably. How come you didn't come with Tad to drop Gretch off yesterday?"

"I had a doctor's appointment."

"Is everything okay?"

"Sweetheart, I'm fine—it's just my yearly physical that I keep cancelling and rescheduling. Your sister keeps me young."

I chuckle, shaking my head. "I'm sure. I'm also sure she's going to make me have gray hair. I can feel it."

My mom gets quiet for a second, and then her soft voice comes through the line. "You remind me so much of your father, especially your laugh." She loves Tad, but I know a part of her will always love my dad. "Okay…anyhoo, have fun with your sister, and we'll see you tomorrow night."

"I love you, Mom."

We hang up, and I check the door then the windows. Yeah, I live in a secure apartment building, but you can never be too careful. I peek in on my sister and see she's still passed out. I bend down and kiss the top of her head.

In my room, I slip out of my jeans and throw on a pair of basketball shorts. Normally I sleep in the nude, but not when my sister's here. After crawling into bed, I stare up at the ceiling. Why did I let Carrie set me up on a blind date? She'd sent me a text earlier with her name—Shayla, but that's all I know. Plus this chick is telling Carrie where and when we should meet? What the fuck? The bitch sounds high maintenance as hell already. I let out a sigh before drifting off to sleep.

***

While I sit in the back of the Uber that's taking me to the restaurant to meet my blind date, my mind is swarming with everything that went down this past week. It started out well enough, with Mom and Tad coming to get Gretchen Sunday night and us going out for pizza as a family. But Mom was in her "why aren't you dating?" mode, which is always followed by, "When are you going to get married and give me grandchildren?" Fuck me, I've never really wanted that. I enjoy the casual flings: no expectations, no promises...easy peasy. Emphasis on the *easy*.

Usually Tad comes to my rescue, reminding my mom that when they met he'd never been married. Out in the parking lot after dinner, I carried my giggling sister over my shoulder to their car. I promised Gretchen we'd talk soon and planned for her to come stay with me again.

As far as work goes, the new guy, Reece, started this week. We hit it off pretty quickly while I gave him a tour of the city, and then to make things even better, I found out he drives a badass Shelby. My 1970 Impala is in the garage across the street from my apartment—I pay a hefty price to keep it there, but at least I know it's safe. I've already invited him over to come take a look at it.

But then shit hit the fan when Delilah was attacked outside of her apartment. Luckily her roommate scared the guy off, but she still ended up in the hospital. She and her unborn son are okay, thankfully. To make the clusterfuck even worse, though, we found out that *Reece* is the father of the baby. Apparently when he came to town to talk to Jack six months ago, he'd hooked up with Delilah without having any clue who she was. They hadn't seen each other since…well, that is until he showed up for his first day. I'm honestly surprised Jack didn't kill him—they must be even closer than I'd guessed.

Now Del's staying with Reece in Oak Park while we try to figure out who hurt her and why. Our whole team has been on edge about it. Delilah is our office's baby sister, and we've all given Jack our word that we won't stop until we find the motherfucker who touched her.

I blow out a deep breath to calm my nerves—just thinking about the dark bruises on Del's face makes me want to punch someone, and that's no mood to start a date in. Earlier I'd picked out my royal blue chambray shirt, the sleeves rolled up to my forearms; a pair of black slacks; and the one pair of dress shoes I own. I keep my blond hair buzzed close to my scalp, so I didn't have to do anything to it.

Once the driver drops me off, I head inside the restaurant, called Starlight. I glance around; I have no idea who I'm looking for. Carrie said that Shayla would know who I was. But why is it such a fucking secret? I kind of have a bad feeling about this, and why wouldn't I? I know her name, and that she's supposedly my type—that's it.

The hostess walks up in the tiniest black dress I've ever seen, and my dick immediately likes what he sees. "Hi, welcome to Starlight. Table for one?" She licks her glossy red lips in what is clearly an invitation. Hmmm…maybe if this date is a bust, she and I can hook up.

"No, darlin', I'm waiting for someone." She gives a fake pout and goes to greet the next customers.

"Erik?" The sultriest voice I've ever heard rises from behind me. After I turn slowly around, my eyes widen. The sexy voice belongs to a woman who is *not* my type at all. She's shorter than the women I tend to go for—*a lot* shorter. And I like blondes, but she's a dark brunette with dark-brown eyes. The red dress she wears hugs her curves—I usually like my women a bit thinner too. I know that makes me sound like a dick, but I can't help who I'm attracted to.

Her light-olive skin tone pops in that dress, and her tits are practically spilling out of the top. They look real too. "Um…*hello*? My face is up here." I look up and she's glaring at me; huh, she's kind of hot when she's pissed. Under her breath, I hear her whisper, "This was a bad idea."

"Sorry. I'm Erik—you must be Shayla." I hold out my hand, and she reluctantly takes it. "It's nice to meet you."

"Yeah, you too." Fuck, her voice is sexy.

The hot hostess leads us to an intimate table in the back. I pull Shayla's chair out for her and push it in for her once she sits. Our hostess hands us our menus and tells us the specials. Yes, my eyes follow her as she walks away from the table. What can I say…it's a bad habit.

"Are you *serious*?" Shayla snaps. I can tell she's pissed—her cheeks are turning red.

I grimace and clear my throat. "Shit, I'm sorry. So, uh…how do you know Carrie?"

She doesn't look up from her menu. "We met at the Starbucks by my job. There wasn't a place to sit and no one would give up their seat, so I slid over and shared the love seat with her. When we started talking, we just really clicked."

"Carrie's a sweetheart, and her husband is a great dude." Shayla, again, doesn't look up from her menu—she just nods her head.

Our waitress comes to our table, and I don't miss the "come fuck me" eyes she's giving me. I ignore her, but when I look at Shayla she's glaring at our waitress, who's oblivious. Why is her irritation making my cock twitch?

Shayla slaps her menu down on the table. "Miss, I hate to interrupt you while you eye-fuck my date, but I'd like to order my meal. Is that okay with you?"

I cough to cover up my laugh, which just pisses Shayla off more, and our waitress's face is beet red. We both order, and the woman hightails it away from our table.

Shayla plays with her napkin, and without thinking, I reach out and grab her hand. "Listen, tonight hasn't started right. Let's do this again. I'm Erik, and you're Shayla."

She studies me for a long time, and then, thankfully, nods her head. "Starting over sounds great. Are you from Chicago?" She takes a sip of her wine.

"No, I'm from Kenosha. My mom, step-dad, and baby sister live there, and I lived there for a short time after I left the Marine Corps. What about you?"

Shayla rubs her arms like she's cold. "I'm from Madison. I moved here two years ago. How old is your sister?"

"Gretchen's fourteen and spoiled, but she's not a brat. I try to have her stay with me at least one weekend a month so we can hang out. This weekend we watched *My Girl* and she cried herself to sleep." I shake my head remembering the way she sobbed…and sobbed.

Shayla gives me a knowing smile. "That is a tearjerker for sure. What made you choose that?"

"My mom suggested it. I know she did it on purpose."

Our waitress interrupts us to drop our food off, hightailing it away from our table like her ass is on fire. Conversation is stalled while we eat. The girl moans around each bite of her steak, and my eyes keep going to her lips. I can picture them wrapped around my dick.

"What do you do?" I ask her while cutting into my T-bone.

"Umm…I'm a temp right now. Not the most glamorous of jobs, but I always get asked to go back to the same places, which is great, and hopefully I'll bide my time and get offered to work one of those places full time." She takes another sip of her wine. "You mentioned your mom and step-dad, but what about your dad?"

That familiar pain hits my chest. Don't get me wrong, I know it was a long time ago, and I still have a lot of amazing memories of my dad, but I miss him every day. I clear the frog in my throat. "He was murdered when I was a boy."

She surprises me by reaching out and grabbing my hand. "Oh God, what happened? Of course I completely understand if you don't want to talk about it."

I squeeze her hand. "It's okay. It was a long time ago." I don't let go of her while I grab my water with my free hand and take a sip. "It was a carjacking. The kid was young and messed up. My mom forgave him a long time ago, and then he became an assistant pastor. He got hired by my step-dad, and that's how Tad and my mom met. I miss my dad every day, but if I hadn't lost my dad, then Mom wouldn't have met Tad, and then we wouldn't have Gretchen."

Where the fuck did *that* all come from?

"That's really amazing that you both were able to forgive that man."

I shrug. "I didn't forgive him for a long time. When I was thirteen, I was a *really* angry kid. I actually went after him one Sunday after church. He let me hit him a few times, too, before my step-dad pulled me off. Tad counseled us together for a while, and after getting to know him, I was able to forgive him. It doesn't mean we're friends, but I don't want to kick his ass anymore."

The mood needs a serious lift. "Anyway. Tell me why you're still single, gorgeous." I give her my trademark cocky grin, which has melted many a pair of panties off of willing females.

She rolls her eyes and drains her glass of wine in one swallow. "Way to ruin a nice moment." Shayla leans forward, and my eyes immediately go to her breasts. "Seriously, dickhead, my eyes are up here." She narrows her eyes at me. "Does that smile really work?"

I stroke the back of her hand with my thumb. She tries to pull it from my grasp, but I hold firm. "It sure does."

Shayla studies me some more, and I don't like it. It's like she can read me and the pain that lives inside me. I hold her stare because I'm not going to let her see it. I've never let *anyone* other than family see it. And by family, I mean my mom, step-dad, and my dad's parents.

I pay the check, and while we're waiting for the waitress to bring my receipt, I get her to agree to go see a movie with me. We decide on the newest Will Ferrell comedy. The waitress brings my receipt to sign, and when I open the little holder, her number is scribbled on a scrap of paper right on top. Before I can grab it, Shayla does, and she waits for the waitress to look our way before making a show of crumpling it up and throwing it in her water glass.

This girl is something else, but why does it turn me on? I get up from my chair and walk around to pull hers out for her—my mom would kick my ass if I didn't do that for a date. With my hand to the small of her back, I lead Shayla out of the restaurant. The theater is a block over, so we decide to walk.

CHAPTER THREE

Shayla

My heart races as we step out into the warm night. I've never seen a more beautiful specimen of a man. I'm five-foot-seven, but next to him I look and feel like a shrimp. His blond hair is clipped short, and it makes his ice-blue eyes stand out. He's a huge guy, like height-wise. He's muscular, but they don't look unnatural. You can just tell he takes *really* good care of his body.

I don't know what's come over me tonight, but the waitress hitting on him in front of me really set me off. Who does that? Yeah, I know I'm plain and a little on the heavier side—or so my ex always told me. On a good day I'm a size ten, but on a bad, a size twelve. But Erik checking her out right in front of me was even worse.

He may be hot, but he's kind of an ass. Who checks out other women when they're on a *date*? Apparently this guy does. Still...I know it's slutty of me, but this guy is huge, so I bet his dick is huge too. I haven't had sex in two years, and this could be my only chance for a while, so I can overlook him being an asshole just this once.

I bet he's good in bed, and I'm sure he's a "wham, bam, thank you ma'am" kind of guy, which is perfect for me. I don't have time to date, nor do I want the trouble. I certainly don't need someone who's probably a cheating scumbag in my life.

I don't know how to flirt or proposition a man, so I make a split decision, grabbing his hand and dragging him into the alley by the restaurant. His eyes widen right before I grab his face and pull him down until our lips meet. Erik doesn't move at first, and I begin to think he's going to pull away.

Instead, it's the complete opposite. He takes control of the kiss and flicks the tip of his tongue against the seam of my lips. I open, letting his tongue dance with mine. God, he can kiss, and I swear I could come right now. His hands grip my hair at the base, and I whimper into his mouth. I can feel Erik's cock through his jeans, and it feels huge.

I've never had "skills" when it comes to men and sex. My ex, when he wasn't cheating on me, complained that I was boring and that I couldn't satisfy him. Right now, though, I don't care. I'm clearing the cobwebs from my vagina, and this man is going to help me do it.

I reach in between us and palm his dick through his pants. His groan tells me he likes it. Pulling back, I look up into his eyes. I give it a squeeze and watch his eyes flare. "I want you to fuck me, please." I know I sound desperate, but I don't care. After tonight, I'm never going to see him again.

He doesn't seem repulsed because he's still

standing in front of me. Erik grabs my chin. "Do you want to come back to my place, or yours?"

"Hotel room," I whisper. Erik nods and grabs my hand. Fate or luck is on my side, and across from the theater is a Holiday Inn.

Hand in hand, he drags me—well, not literally—toward the hotel. Luckily there are rooms available. Erik doesn't let me pay, and I don't argue because I just want to get to the good stuff. In the elevator, the only sound is our breathing and my pounding heart.

We reach our floor and he drags me off into the hallway. My nerves are getting the better of me, but I'm not backing out—not when I can feel how wet my panties are.

He uses the keycard to open the door and pulls me inside. Erik's hands go to my ass, and he lifts me effortlessly. I slam my lips down on his, and our tongues begin to duel. I pull back and he nips my lower lip, licking the sting away before his lips travel along my jaw to my ear.

We're moving through the darkened room until he falls on his back onto the bed, never once taking his lips from my neck. Erik's hands slide down the back of my dress until he reaches the hem. He slowly pulls it up around my hips.

Erik rolls us so he's on top of me and between my legs. My breath leaves me in pants as I stare up at him. He reaches out and strokes my lower lip with his thumb. "Tell me what you want?"

I bite my lower lip. What *do* I want? No one has ever asked me that. Taking a deep breath, I say, "I want you to lick me." I want to squeal right now because I can't believe I just said that.

"Let's get you out of this dress," he whispers. Erik's voice is deeper—sexier.

He immediately zeroes in on the zipper, making quick work of pulling it down. Erik grabs the top of my dress and yanks it down my body, leaving me in only my black lace panties.

I don't miss the hungry look in his eyes as he stares at my breasts. They're D cups, and sometimes I wish they were perkier than they actually are. He doesn't seem to mind, though, because his lips wrap around one nipple, sucking it into his mouth. I arch my back as pleasure shoots through me. He rubs his pants-covered dick against my clit, and I moan.

He switches to the other nipple, giving it the same treatment. Erik dips his fingers into my panties, and he moans when they slide across my wet lips. He pushes one finger inside me and embarrassingly, I begin to come immediately.

Erik pulls his finger out and brings it to his lips, licking my cum off. He bends down, kissing me and letting me taste myself on his lips. Before the pulsing in my pussy stops, I reach up and rip open Erik's pants while he takes his shirt off. He grabs a strip of condoms out of his pants, pulls one off, and throws the rest on the bed next to me.

With quick moves, he rips my panties away from my body, leaving me naked and exposed to his gaze. His eyes roam over my body and he licks his lips. "So fucking sexy," he whispers almost to himself.

Erik quickly climbs off the bed, takes off his pants, and chucks them on the other bed. If I thought he was hot before, he's even hotter completely naked. His cock is long and thick, standing tall against his stomach—I just *knew* it was going to be huge, and he doesn't disappoint. He climbs back on the bed and rolls a condom on before moving closer to the apex of my thighs.

I watch as he grips his dick by the base. He rubs it through my juices and then lines it up with my opening. In one swift move, he thrusts inside me, burying himself to the hilt. I cry out and feel myself being stretched to the max.

He grabs one thigh, pulling it up and over his hip—opening me up more to him. Erik pulls almost all the way out then pushes slowly back inside. He holds my gaze in an intense stare that makes my belly quiver.

"Fuck baby, you're so tight." He groans before bending his head down, kissing my lips gently before he starts thrusting his cock into me over and over. The ache below begins to build again, and I welcome it. I plan on milking every orgasm I can out of him to tide me over for a *long* time.

With every roll of his hips, I shudder in his arms. I grip his ass cheeks, and they're just as firm and hard as I imagined they were when I checked him out earlier. They clench and relax over and over as he pounds into me. He hits a spot deep inside that has me groaning into his mouth. Over and over he hits it until I'm silently screaming against his mouth as the most intense orgasm I've ever had hits me.

I want to break the connection between us, but he holds me captive with his stare. He grabs my other thigh, pushing it back until I'm almost bent in half. Erik begins to pound into me with an almost brutal pace. Then he suddenly pulls out. Before I can protest, he picks me up, wrapping my legs around his hips and impaling me on his cock. There, in the middle of the bed, on his knees, he bounces me up and down on his cock.

"Oh God, oh *fuuuuck*," I groan. I've never felt this kind of pleasure in all my life.

He nips at my earlobe and then whispers against my ear, "Baby, you feel so fucking good. Are you going to come for me? Are you going to come all over my cock?"

I shudder violently as I come. Erik quiets my screams with his mouth on mine and picks up the pace until he holds me down tight as he pushes up, burying his dick so far in me it's borderline painful as he groans into my neck. He holds me just like that for a while, and I drape my arms over his shoulders.

Erik kisses my forehead, and for a second I let myself pretend that someone like him would truly want someone like me. He's way out of my league, but at least for one night I get to experience a pleasure I've never felt before. My ex never cared if I came, and he said it was my fault. At least tonight I feel good—desirable. This will have to last me awhile.

***

The room is pitch black, and Erik's arm is draped heavily over my waist. His hand still cups my pussy while he snores softly behind me. How many times did we have sex or give each other oral?

I didn't think it was possible to have that many orgasms, but I lost count after the second round.

I need to get out of here before he wakes up—I don't want to see the awkwardness or feel his regret. It would be humiliating if I had to watch him try to escape me like I'm some kind of disease.

Lifting his arm, I slide out from under him and gingerly climb out of bed. I watch him to make sure he doesn't wake, and when he just rolls over and begins to snore again, I let out the breath I was holding. I pick up my dress, slip it on, and then slide my feet into my heels. With one last look at Erik, I grab my wristlet and walk out of the hotel room.

The Uber driver is quiet, thankfully. I'm not in the mood to talk. I just want to hold onto my memories of tonight. The driver drops me off in front of my place, and he tells me he's going to sit in his car and wait for me to get inside. I thank him and hurry up the walk to my door.

I open the door to my apartment and find Luna asleep on the sofa with Grant and her two girls asleep on the floor under a pile of blankets. I kick off my heels then head into the bathroom to brush out my hair, wash my face, and brush my teeth. In my room, I change into an old Lady Gaga t-shirt and a pair of knit shorts.

When I head back into the living room, I find Luna stretching with her arms above her head. She turns toward me. "How was your date?"

I sit down next to her. "I don't know why Carrie thought we'd hit it off. He's gorgeous—I mean, so sexy he should be a fitness model or on the cover of a romance novel. Our waitress practically climbed onto his lap. And he was so freaking cocky, and he spent more time staring at my tits than my face, but then he shared about losing his dad and got sweet, and went right back to being a douche. It gave me whiplash."

Luna looks me over. "Okay, he may be a douche, but why do you have a love bite on your neck?"

My face heats up immediately. "I haven't had sex since Ryan, and I didn't think I'd get the chance to sleep with someone like him. I jumped him outside of the restaurant."

"Okay first, I want to know why you think you wouldn't hit it off. So he's gorgeous...have you looked in a mirror? You're *beautiful*—you've got a great body and a beautiful soul." I shake my head, but she continues talking. "You haven't told me a lot about your ex, but he really did a number on you. Honey, you may not see it, but *I* do."

I grab her and me some blankets and pillows, and we sleep on the couch and love seat, which we've done before when Rocco was out of town for work and she didn't want to be alone.

When I wake up, I find all three kids are watching cartoons with the volume down low. Sitting up, I cover my mouth as I yawn and then get up. I stroke my hand over Grant and the girls' heads; they all smile at me before I head down the hall to the bathroom. After finishing, I wash my hands and brush my teeth.

When I step back into the living room, Luna is awake with her youngest snuggled in her lap. "Coffee?" I ask.

"Coffee sounds great."

In the kitchen I start the coffeemaker, and while the coffee is brewing, I grab a bottle of ibuprofen and shake a couple pills into my hand. I pop them in my mouth and wash them down with some water. Earlier when I'd gone to the bathroom, I'd noticed that my vagina was freaking sore, but considering I'd never had that much sex, I shouldn't have been surprised—plus, his dick was *huge*.

Of course my whole body aches from using muscles I don't think I've ever used before. I shake off the thoughts of Erik. I'll never see him again, but I'll at least have material to use when I masturbate.

I grab the ingredients I need and begin whipping up my famous chocolate chip pancakes. Luna joins me and we work side by side to feed the troops. Once we're finished, we both lean against the counter watching Grant, Lennon, and Starr all wolf down their food.

After breakfast, Luna and the girls head home and I have Grant take a shower. I try to let him be a big boy and wash himself, but I'm never too far to help and make sure he gets all his little nooks and crannies. Once he gets out I start a load of laundry, and we spend the rest of the day curled up on the sofa watching every Marvel movie we own.

It's Grant and I against the world, and that's the way we like it.

***

It's been two weeks since my date with Erik, and life has continued as normal. Well, except for the fact that every freaking night I dream about the sexy douchebag: the way he made me feel, the way his dick felt inside me, and everything in between.

I've avoided Carrie for the most part, just because I don't want her to think badly of me for sleeping with Erik on our first and only date. She's also had her baby, so it's been very easy to make up excuses for not bothering her. Of course I'm now going to be filling in for her at the company she works at.

I heard from the manager, Delilah, and met with her. She's a young, pregnant blonde who's so welcoming. She hired me on the spot and had me fill out all the forms. Insurance will kick in right away, which I'm happy about. I've had Medicaid since I moved here and I don't have a lot of options for Grant.

Delilah showed me pictures of Carrie's bundle of joy, and of course my beautiful friend looks fabulous for just having had a baby. Leif is a gorgeous little boy, but I'm not surprised.

She gave me my keycards to get onto the elevator and into the back of the office. I'll be greeting clients when they come, accepting deliveries, helping with billing, and whatever else is needed.

Now I'm heading toward the office for my first day. After I get off the L, I head down the stairs to the street and adjust my messenger bag over my shoulder. I hope I'm dressed okay. It's warm out, so I opted for a short-sleeved shirt dress the color of watermelon, and a wide belt around my waist. My espadrille wedges are a combination of the same watermelon color, lime green, and cornflower blue.

I reach the building, step inside, and head toward the elevator. I swipe my card and the doors open; they take me up to my floor. When I step off, I take a deep breath. On the desk is a vase full of daisies and a card with my name on it.

Shayla,

I just wanted to welcome you to Rogue Security. We're excited to have you join us.

Sincerely,

Delilah

This right here is why I'm glad I've come to work here. I stick the card back in the envelope and slip it in my bag. I grab my lunch and my card to get into the back. The closer I get to the break room, the sounds of deep male voices get louder, causing butterflies to take flight in my belly.

When I reach the doorway, both men turn toward me. One is African-American with a ripped, muscular build and tattoos covering his arms. The other man is Caucasian and lean with light-brown hair, green eyes, peaches-and-cream skin, and a closely trimmed beard.

"Um...hi there," I say. "I'm Shayla. I'm Carrie's replacement."

The bearded man stands up first and holds his hand out to me. "I'm Dalton." *Oh*, he's British. I like that.

The other guy stands up next, and I shake his hand as well. "I'm Marcus. It's nice meeting you.

34

I'm the resident bounty hunter, and I'll actually be leaving in about an hour to go after a skip. If you're taking on Carrie's duties, you'll email me any info that I need while I'm out on the road."

I nod. "Okay, great. What about you, Dalton?"

"I help run surveillance with one of the other guys. I'm also a martial arts expert." Marcus groans and then walks away. I raise my brow at Dalton. "He's just jealous because I could kick his ass."

"I don't think so," I hear Marcus holler from somewhere in the office.

After putting my lunch in the refrigerator, I pour myself a cup of coffee. A few of the other men show up, and Dalton introduces me to them. They're all friendly and definitely enjoy razzing each other.

Once Delilah shows up, we head to her office. "Thank you for the flowers," I say. "That's so sweet of you."

"You're welcome. We're outnumbered here so we have to stick together."

In her office, we go over my duties again, and she hands me printed-out instructions on how to do a lot of Carrie's tasks. "These look great."

"I'll sit with you for a while today. The phones are easy, and our computer programs we use are easy too."

"Sounds great." She leads me out to my desk and helps get my account set up. Delilah has me send out an email to all the employees with my contact information. Once that's done, we begin our day. When the phones aren't ringing, we check everyone's calendars and make sure no one double-booked themselves and that no meetings will cause conflicts with clients.

The morning goes by quickly, and several of the guys stop over to introduce themselves and welcome me to the company. I've never seen so many good-looking guys in one space. I even got to meet Carrie's husband when he stopped in to bring me cookies that Carrie made for me as a welcome gift. Again, another reason I'm so happy I came here.

During my first break, I step outside to call Luna and check on Grant. He's fine, and they're working on writing their letters. Luna was a teacher before she became a stay-at-home mom, so she's been working with him. I tell her about my morning, and she's happy I'm enjoying it.

I take the elevator back upstairs, and when I step back into the office, I find a man leaning against my desk talking to Delilah. She sees me and smiles. "Oh, hey—Erik, this is Shayla."

I freeze as he slowly stands up straight and turns around to face me. Oh...My...God. What is he doing here? I wipe the shock from my face and walk toward him. "It's...nice to meet you."

He moves closer. "You left without so much as a 'have a nice life.' What gives?"

I glance nervously at Delilah before whispering, "We're *not* talking about this right now."

"Are you married? Is that why?" His blue eyes flare, and I want to smack him in his beautiful face.

"*Of course* I'm not married," I hiss. "I'm no cheater." He looks relieved.

"Umm...is everything okay?" Delilah's standing

next to me now. "Do you guys know each other?"

"No," I blurt, just as Erik says, "Yes."

"Is this going to be a problem?" Delilah asks, looking between the two of us.

Shaking my head, I look at him and then at her. "No, of course not. I apologize. This isn't very professional."

I head back to the desk and Delilah sits down next to me.

Erik stops next to me. "We need to talk later." He then heads into the back.

It's probably not a good idea, but I decide to tell Delilah the deal. "So…Carrie set us up on a blind date, and umm…yeah." I say nothing more about that, but I look at her. "I promise this won't affect my working here."

She grabs my hand. "Okay. Just *please* let me know if things get awkward for either of you."

A while later, Erik comes back out and I can feel his eyes on me, but I choose to ignore him. Every so often, I shoot him the occasional dirty look while he sits on the love seat staring at me. In the meantime, I meet Reece, Delilah's "boyfriend," although I'm not exactly sure what he is, except that he's the father of her baby. I also meet her dad, who is a lot younger than I pegged her father to be, but he was also young when she was born.

They're both very nice and welcoming. After they're all gone and I'm alone, I'm finally able to take a deep breath.

CHAPTER FOUR

Erik

She's here—I've finally found her, and she's going to be working with me. The morning after our date, I'd woken up alone and pissed. That was some of the best sex I've ever had, and she disappeared after it without a trace. Carrie wouldn't give me any information, and I couldn't badger her about it—otherwise Egan would've kicked my ass.

Who fucks so much their dick gets sore? Apparently me, because my dick was sore for days, and fuck me, I couldn't get the taste of her off my tongue. I didn't want to, either—I loved having the reminder. I've jerked off to the memory of her tight little pussy more times than I care to admit.

Normally I'd wake up from a night of sex and *I'd* be the one to leave in the night. But I'd never felt that sort of connection with anyone before—I hadn't been *looking* for any sort of connection, either. But when I looked into her eyes, it was like I could see all the way to her soul. I know that sounds cheesy as fuck, but I don't care.

38

It was the last time we fucked before falling asleep. I'd been sitting up in the bed, and she'd had her feet on the mattress next to my hips. Shayla rocked and rolled her hips while bouncing up and down on my cock. Our eyes locked, and something inside of me snapped. I'd grabbed her face, bringing her down to meet me in an urgent possession of lips, tongues, and teeth.

As soon as I felt the beginnings of her orgasm, I flipped us over and began pounding into her at a brutal pace. Had I not been wearing a condom, I would've definitely knocked her up. After we finished, I'd barely gotten the condom off before we both passed out.

Now she's sitting at the front desk, looking more gorgeous than I remember. She better not try to leave before we have the chance to talk. Does she realize that now that I've found her, she's not getting away from me that easily? Am I saying that I want a relationship with her? No, but I want to spend some time with her to see if the connection is purely sexual…or something else.

Fuuuuck, why do I care? I'm Mr. Carefree, bang whoever I want, whenever I want. Maybe because she was refreshing—she gave as good as she got in bed. My usual type only wants to do it in angles that make them look good, but not Shayla—she fucked me like I fucked her. She was wild and uninhibited. Fucking her was fun, and I don't think I've ever said that…ever.

Reece follows me into my office and sits down across from my desk. I look up at him as I sit. "*What?* Just say it." In the short time he's been here, Reece has become a good buddy.

"She's pretty," he says simply. I nod. "It's obvious she's got you all twisted up. What're you going to do?"

I shake my head. "I've got no clue. I don't do relationships."

"I felt the same way until Delilah and I reconnected. We really haven't crossed into relationship territory, at least not yet, but we will."

Luckily, he changes the subject. We've been working together going through security tapes of places near Delilah's apartment, looking for any clues leading to who might've attacked her. We make plans for the next day to go over the newest footage. I'm spending the rest of my day doing paperwork on cases that I've finished and getting my hours turned in so I get paid.

Shayla has ignored me all day, which had been easy for her to do because Delilah has been working with her. But Delilah's in her office right now, which means Shayla is alone. Without a second thought, I head out to the reception area.

She's typing away on the computer with earbuds in. I grab a chair and slide in close to her. Shayla freezes and turns toward me. She pulls her earbuds out. "What?"

"Have dinner with me, or at least a drink? Let's talk." Her light floral scent wraps around me, making my dick hard. Now I'm aching to be inside of her again.

She shakes her head. "There's nothing to talk about. It was one night." She turns back to the computer.

I lean in close, caging her in. "It was *not* just one night, and you know it. You know we connected, and I don't connect with *anyone*." My breath hits her neck, and I don't miss the goosebumps that pop up all over her arms. "That was the best fucking sex I've ever had."

She pretends like she's not affected by my words, but I don't miss the way her breathing quickens. Shayla leans toward me. "You're full of shit," she whispers harshly. "I know what I look like compared to the hostess at the restaurant that you couldn't take your eyes off of. I've been down that road before, and I don't plan on doing it again."

"Yes, you're not my usual type, but you're beautiful—especially when you're riding my cock." Her cheeks turn pink. I absently play with the ends of her hair.

Reece comes out, interrupting us. It gives Shayla time to ignore me and put up her defenses. That's okay, because my mom's always told me I'm stubborn. I'll wear her down until we can at least fuck each other out of our systems.

Shayla makes her escape with Delilah and Reece. I'll let her run now, but she'll see soon enough that we've got some incredible chemistry, and we owe it to ourselves to see what could happen.

***

The past week I've been avoiding the office. I'm trying not to be in Shayla's space because if I'm there, then I want to be close to her. Delilah pulled me aside Shayla's first week and said I was coming on too strongly—her words, not Shayla's. I know I can be a little over the top, but that's just my personality.

Then *Reece* pulled me into his office. He'd leaned against his desk and crossed his arms over his chest, his eyebrows raised. "So what's *really* the deal with you and Shayla? And not the bullshit version, the truth. It's easy to see there's a lot of tension on her end, and I'm not just talking about the sexual kind."

So I told him about our date—every little detail, and by just saying it out loud I was actually a little embarrassed. For so long I haven't given a shit about the women I've taken to bed, and now that I do, my past behavior is coming back to bite me in the ass. I could tell by the grimace on Reece's face as I shared all the nitty gritty that he agreed.

The question of the day is: What makes *Shayla* so special? She's attractive, sure, but I would never seek out a woman like her in any other situation. It's probably because no other woman—well, except Del and the females I'm related to—has ever called me on my shit, and Shayla did it the day we met. It was hot as fuck too.

"I've got to prove to her that I'm not a douche," I told Reece. "Well...I'm *still* a douche, but I want to prove I'm a good guy too." My throat closed up as I thought of what she'd said when I confronted her that first day at the office. "She thinks I'm a cheating scumbag. I may be a lot of things, but I'm sure as fuck not that."

"You *are* a good guy—I just think you need to

make her see that, without being obnoxious about it. Show her the Erik that has his baby sister over for sleepovers and watches over his buddies' wives."

I left Reece's office shortly after that, and I've avoided Shayla ever since. Just like both Reece and Del told me to do, I'm giving her the space to make her own decision.

It's been easy keeping myself busy, though—I've got a couple of cases that I've picked up this week. Of course, this coming Friday we have a staff meeting, so I'll see her then.

I stop at the store on my way home and grab groceries so I can do some meal prep for the rest of the week. I keep up a pretty strict diet and exercise regimen. Looking this good takes hard work and dedication, and I don't miss the appreciative glances I get from female customers. The girl who rings me up is red-faced and flustered while I try to talk to her.

When she hands me my receipt, I give her a wink. "Thanks, doll." I hear her giggle as I grab my bags, stick them in my cart, and head out of the store.

Once I load the back of my Explorer, I climb inside, lean my head back, and groan. That shit is *exactly* why Shayla is resistant to us going out again, but it's just automatic sometimes. Fuck, I need to get my shit together. My phone rings and I see my sister's face smiling at me. It's a picture from when she'd made me take her to Brookfield Zoo. I swipe the screen and hold the phone to my ear. "What's up, baby sis?"

"Hi, big brother. Mom wants you to come for

dinner Friday night. Can you? We're celebrating me getting on the honor roll." My baby sister is so fucking smart. I'm so proud of her.

"Sure thing, I wouldn't miss it. Maybe I'll stay the night and we can go eat at Flip's for breakfast." It's been her favorite place to eat since she was little. They have cinnamon rolls the size of someone's head. If I eat there I'll pretty much have to increase my workouts for about a week after, but to hang with her, it's worth it.

"Yes!" Her excitement makes me smile. I hear her tell Mom that I'll be coming and staying overnight. "I can't wait to see you."

"You just saw me a couple of weeks ago."

"I know, but I miss you. We have so much fun together." She knows how to bring me to my knees.

I coddle her, I know, but I've loved that little monster from the first time I held her in my arms. It was really odd to be almost out of high school with a toddler at home, but she made life interesting. "I miss you too, kid. I'll see you Friday."

After we hang up, I head home and make two trips to get my groceries upstairs. It takes me a couple of hours to finish prepping my meals before I head to bed so I can hit the gym first thing in the morning. After a good night's sleep, I change into my workout clothes and head out.

I'm finishing a set of back squats when I spot Heather and Lacey—they're best friends who do *everything* together, and I mean *everything*. Now, *they* are my usual type: tall, leggy blondes, fake tits, and pencil-thin bodies. Now a curvy brunette is monopolizing my thoughts.

They come prancing over and my dick does nothing—nada…zilch.

"Hey, Erik," Heather purrs. "We saw you and had to stop by and see if you wanted to come over? We haven't seen you in forever."

A part of me wants to say yes because that's what I do, but my dick doesn't seem to care that I've been inside both of these women and have seen them fuck each other. All my dick cares about is Shayla and the way she rode me like a fucking, bucking bronco.

"Ladies, I would love to, but I can't. Maybe some other time?" Not likely if I have it my way and can get Shayla to quit blowing me off.

They both pout, but give me a kiss on each cheek before walking away hand in hand. I can only shake my head as I move on to my next set.

After my workout, I grab a protein shake and head out to my Explorer. Once I get home, I shower and then get dressed for the day. My phone pings, and I take it off the charger.

Jack: Can you come in today? I want to go over Delilah's case.

"Fuck." I sigh before picking up my phone. "So much for avoiding the office."

Erik: Yeah, I'm on my way.

I slip on my motorcycle boots and head out the door.

After parking in the garage, I climb out of my

SUV and head to the elevator. I ride it up to our floor, and when the door opens, I spot Shayla sitting behind the desk. She watches me as I walk toward the door that leads into the back. When I reach her, I give two quick knocks on her desk with my fist and lift my chin in greeting. "Good morning."

In the back, I grab a cup of coffee and a banana before heading into the conference room. It's just Jack, Reece, Egan, and me. Before Jack starts, Shayla comes in with a notepad. She takes the seat next to mine, and her familiar scent wraps around me like a cloak. I shift in my seat, thankful the table top is hiding my erection from the guys.

Jack talks to us about all the information he's found, which unfortunately isn't much. I've helped Marcus review past case files just to make sure this isn't a revenge thing, but everyone's had alibis. It's like whoever did it just...vanished.

Shayla scribbles on her pad next to me, and I watch her out of the corner of my eye. Her hair is up today, and images assail me as I think about kissing that neck and nipping at her sensitive flesh. What the fuck is wrong with me?

I've prided myself on my ability to never get attached. I'm Mr. Good Time Guy, but Shayla calls to me in a different way. She calls to me in a way that I'm not comfortable with, and I have to know if it's just sexual or not.

Once Jack dismisses us, I get up and am out of the conference room before Shayla is even out of her chair. In my office, I sit behind my desk and log into my laptop. I'm in the middle of going through my emails when there's a knock on my open door.

I assume it's Jack or Reece, but I'm surprised to find Shayla standing there looking uncertain. She's wearing a form-fitting gray dress with a lime-green cardigan over it. Her makeup is light, and she's incredibly beautiful.

I don't say anything at first; I just watch her fidget nervously in the doorway, but I don't make her wait long. "Did you need something?"

She steps closer to my desk. "Are you okay? Did I upset you?" Shayla wrings her hands in front of her.

Okay, I wasn't expecting that. I get up from my desk and don't miss the subtle flinch from her. Who hurt her? It's obvious *someone* did. I've always been very observant—it's always been easy to pick up someone else's subtle cues. "I'm fine, sweetheart. No, you didn't upset me. I was just giving you space."

Do I see relief on her face? Why does she even care? I reach behind her and push the door shut. Every instinct I have is telling me to back her up against the wall and plunder her mouth, but instead I cup her face. Her eyes flare right before I slam my mouth down on hers. Immediately her unique flavor explodes on my tongue. A deep groan escapes from my chest, and my cock gets hard...*again*.

All too soon, she steps away from me, and before I can say anything, she's out of my office. I rub a hand over my head and sigh. "Well, that wasn't backing off." *Fuck me,* this woman has got me acting fucking stupid.

By the end of the day, I'm mentally spent. Every time she was even in the same vicinity as me, I couldn't think and couldn't focus. The guys must've been able to pick up on my mood, because they all avoided me. The only one who didn't was Delilah, but working with a bunch of bossy men has toughened up her skin; she dishes it out now as good as she takes it.

Heading out, I stop the elevator from shutting with my hand. When I step on, I find Shayla in the cab, typing something on her phone. When she looks up, she smiles nervously at me. "How was the rest of your day?"

"Good, thanks. You?" Could we *get* any more awkward? Fuck, I'm like some high school kid who's never even talked to a woman, let alone seen one naked.

"It was great, thanks."

We reach the parking garage, and I watch her give me a bit of a wave before heading toward the exit. "Where are you going?" I call out.

"Taking the L."

I jog toward her. "Let me give you a ride."

"Thanks, but it seriously isn't that far. I do it all the time." She continues walking away from me.

"The protector in me can't in good conscience let you." I move to stand in front of her. "Please, let me do this."

She finally agrees and lets me lead her to my Explorer. I help her inside, and then she gives me her address. After plugging it into my GPS, we head toward her place. Out of the corner of my eye, I watch her pick at her nails and stare out the passenger window. I hate that I make her nervous. That was never my intention, and I hope I've

48

somewhat shown that over the past week or so. Of course, the strongest impression she's had of me so far is that I can be a selfish pig.

"How do you like your job?" *See*, I can be a nice guy.

She turns to look at me. "I love it. Everyone has been great."

"I'm glad, sweetheart."

We're both silent on the way toward her apartment. It's a companionable silence, and when I pull up to her building, it's one of those apartments that look like a huge house. There are usually three units, one on top of the other. As soon as I slow to a stop, she says a quick, "thank you" and hops out.

In her heels she expertly runs up her sidewalk to the side entrance and disappears inside. I don't move right away—a part of me is hoping to catch a glimpse of her inside, but of course I don't know which apartment is actually hers.

With a sigh, I throw my SUV in drive and head toward the gym. I need to burn off this pent-up energy.

CHAPTER FIVE

Shayla

I climb out of the Uber, thanking the driver for the ride. As soon as I reach the door, it opens and Carrie greets me with baby Leif in her arms. I couldn't avoid her any longer, plus I was dying to get my hands on her baby.

"Hi, momma!" I kiss her cheek, and then Leif's forehead. Once we're inside, she hands him over and we sit side by side on their sofa. "You look fantastic."

Carrie smooths a hand over her hair. "Thanks. I'm so exhausted and overwhelmed a lot, but *so* freaking happy."

I remember what it was like after I had Grant. What kind of a man gets jealous of the love the mother of their child shows that child? Ryan made me feel guilty all the time for wanting to spend more time with Grant than I did with him. Of course he didn't mind when Grant wanted his daddy.

Grant was who kept me sane while I ate the shit that Ryan dished out. "Shayla?"

"Oh gosh, I'm sorry. Listen, there's something I need to tell you…well, a couple of things." I stroke Leif's cheek with my finger. "I have a son." Her eyes widen. "I didn't mean to keep it from you, but…*ugh*…I was in an abusive marriage, and when Grant was three, he walked in on Ryan hurting me badly enough there was blood. Since then, he's not really comfortable around men at first." I shake my head. "I can't believe I just spit that all out."

Instead of looking at me with pity, she smiles and grabs my hand. "So you're obviously one of the strongest women I know, because you're here and obviously not with that monster. Where's your little boy?"

"He's at my neighbor's—she watches him while I work." I grab my phone out of my purse and show her a picture of Grant and me from a few weeks ago.

"He looks just like you!" Carrie says. "He's beautiful. Next time you come, you should bring him." She gets up and grabs us each a bottle of water out of her kitchen. "So…tell me about your date with Erik. Don't think I haven't noticed that you've been avoiding me since."

"Why did you set me up with him? He's so beautiful and muscular, and women *flock* to him." I glance up at her. "He was an asshole the whole time we were at dinner, flirting with the hostess and staring at my boobs, but I still had sex with him. Lots and lots of amazing sex, and then I took off while he slept. *Please* don't think poorly of me. I've never done that before."

She looks at me closely. "Okay, I want you to

listen to me, and listen good: You are the *perfect* woman for him. I can't really explain it, but once you get past that douchey exterior, there's a big teddy bear in there. I happen to think you're the best person to pull that side out of him." She shakes her head. "I know we haven't known each other long, but I'd never set you up with someone who I thought would carelessly break your heart. He *is* a good guy—trust me on that."

I let her words swirl around in my brain for a bit. She really thinks Erik is that great? That *I'm* that great *for* him? It doesn't make sense. What am I missing? Sure, he told me about his sister and what happened to his dad, but just as quickly as that vulnerability appeared, he'd shelved it.

I'd definitely noticed when he backed off at work, though. And for him to say he was giving me space before kissing me like that *and* offering to drive me home…it's like he's two different people at once. But maybe that means he's trying, at least.

My stomach drops. But what does it matter, if all the effort in the world won't make me the kind of woman he *really* wants?

Carrie kisses her son's forehead, and then looks back up at me. "Yes, he's good-looking, but so are you—inside and out. Don't think I would *ever* judge you for enjoying yourself. Are you an adult?" I nod. "Did you force him to have sex with you?"

Shaking my head, I mutter, "I…kind of jumped him."

Carrie throws her head back and laughs. "That's understandable. Sorry I didn't tell you he worked with me and that you'd see him afterward—I didn't want that to color your impression of him. Are you going to go out with him again?"

I shrug. "We've kissed a couple of times. It's just...I don't know if I want to or not. Grant is skittish around men, and honestly, I've got too much baggage. He could have it easy with other women, I'm sure. Plus, he hasn't really even talked to me much. I mean, he kissed me yesterday in his office, but he hasn't asked me out since my first day, and I said no then."

"Ask *him* out. Take him out to dinner and just talk to him. Or hell, just bang each other, because I may be married, and my husband is no slouch, but Erik is *seriously fine*."

Ohhh...why does that make me feel so crazy? Of course I know she's joking when she winks at me. "I don't know...maybe." I smile down at the sleeping baby in my arms. When I was younger, I wanted a houseful of children that I would shower with love, but then that dream died when Ryan started hitting me. I doubt I'll ever get married again, which in turn means no children.

I've had my heart broken enough by my ex-husband...I don't think I could ever have a relationship with someone who would blatantly flirt with other women in front of me, no matter what Carrie says.

I stay for a little longer, but then the sweet little boy begins getting upset, wanting his mama. I order an Uber and stand up when I see it pull up out front. "Thanks for letting me come visit. Sorry I was avoiding you."

Carrie lays Leif down in the bassinet in the

living room and comes over to wrap her arms around me. "Don't be sorry, and don't think I'd ever judge you for anything. Don't forget: Next time you come, you better bring Grant with you."

I only nod, because emotions clog my throat. For so long I was so lonely—Ryan made me stop talking to all my friends, and even my family turned their backs on me. Now, I've got Luna, Rocco, Carrie, and Delilah. It feels good to be rebuilding my tribe. "I promise I'll bring him."

She pulls back and smiles at me. "Good."

On my way back to the office my thoughts wander, and I don't know what I'm going to do about Erik. When I arrive, I thank the driver and climb out of the car. I head inside through the front doors, saying hello to the security guard. At the elevators, I use my card to get on the employee elevator and ride it up to my floor.

I smile when I see Delilah behind the desk. "Hey, thanks for covering for me," I say.

"You're welcome. How was Carrie?" She stands up and walks around the desk. Delilah is all belly, and totally cute. Reece is a big dude, and I can only imagine how big that baby is going to be. Grant was seven pounds when he was born and absolutely perfect.

"She was good. She's got that new mommy glow. It won't be long before you have it too."

Delilah smiles as she rubs a hand over her belly. "I can't wait. I'm excited to meet this little boy."

I take my spot behind the desk and put my purse in the bottom drawer.

I'm just going through my email when my phone

vibrates. I pick it up and see Luna's name on the screen. "Hey Luna, is everything okay?"

"Hey, I just wanted to let you know: Grant just threw up, but he seems fine. He's not running a fever, and said his stomach didn't hurt anymore. My guess is something just didn't sit right in his belly."

Every now and then this happens. "Okay, do you want me to come get him?"

"Honestly, he seems fine. He's eating some homemade applesauce right now. I'll call you if any of that changes." She is the absolute best.

"If you're sure. Can you hand the phone to him?" I hear rustling around.

"Hi, Mommy. I frew up."

"Hey, my little Grunt. That's what Luna said, and that your tummy is better. Tonight we'll have chicken noodle soup and a *Cars* marathon, okay? Love you."

"Okay, love you."

Luna takes the phone back. "Whatever you told him has him smiling ear to ear. We'll let you get back to work—and again, I'll call if he gets worse."

"Okay, thanks girl." I disconnect and leave my phone on my desk, just in case.

"You have a kid?" I spin around to find Erik standing next to my desk, staring at me.

I nod, my heart in my throat. "Y-Yes. He's five. His name's Grant."

"Where's his father?"

I avoid looking him in the eye. "He's…not in the picture."

"Do you have any pictures of him?" Why am I surprised he's asking to see him?

I pick up my phone again, and after opening the photo app I hand it to him. I watch him swipe to the left, looking at the pictures of my reason for living. He smiles and shows me the picture he's looking at now.

It's from Grant's fifth birthday breakfast. Grant was at the kitchen table with a pile of pancakes covered in chocolate sauce and whipped cream. Lucifer was in his arms, and I was squatting down next to him. We both had party hats on. "That was a good day," I tell him. "That's our cat, Lucifer."

He raises a brow. "Lucifer?"

I nod. "Yep, he was a rescue, and at first he hissed at me whenever I tried to hold him—Grant was the only one who could. Luckily, he finally warmed up to me, and now I can't keep him away from me." Erik hands me back my phone. I turn back to my computer, assuming that he's going to walk away—nothing kills the mood for a bachelor like talking about kids.

"Have you eaten lunch?" he asks instead. I shake my head, and notice it's already noon. "Have lunch with me?"

I remember what Luna and Carrie both said—this is the perfect chance to at least get to know him. If *he's* trying, I can at least try too. "Yes, sure, that sounds great." He looks surprised that I said yes, but he quickly covers it. I email Delilah to let her know I'm stepping out for lunch so she can cover the front desk again. After logging out, I grab my purse and sling it over my shoulder.

Erik's hand rests on my lower back as we head to the elevator. Neither of us says a word as we take it down to the parking garage. He holds out a key fob and the lights flash on his Explorer. Erik is definitely a gentleman, opening my door for me and helping me inside.

That familiar spicy scent of his wraps around me, and I sink further into the soft leather seat. His door opens and he climbs inside. We reach the exit of the garage. "Does Thai sound okay?"

"That sounds great."

The host leads us to a booth, and Erik sits across from me. His legs are so long that they take up all the space under the table. I cross my legs and rest my hands in my lap. Our waiter stops by and takes our drink order. Once he walks away, Erik turns and gives me that damn cocky grin of his.

"Tell me about Grant. What's he like?"

I can't help but smile widely. I love my boy so much. "He's amazing. He loves to read, and my neighbor upstairs watches him—he helps her with her little girls." I look down at the table, then back up at him. "Grant is shy around people he doesn't know, but that's a story for another day."

Luckily the waiter comes and Erik asks if he can order for me. I agree, and my mouth waters as I listen to him order enough food for a small army.

"Tell me about Gretchen."

"She's amazing too. When my mom had her, I was sixteen and not really thrilled about having a baby in the house, but the first time I held her, it was fucking *magical*. I know that hurts my street cred." He laughs to himself, and I love the deep, rich sound. "Or my massive sex appeal." Erik gives me a cocky wink.

Our waiter brings our plates, and my eyes widen as I take in the food that he sets in the middle of the table; he places a couple of empty plates on the end. Once he's gone, I look at Erik. "Um, this is a *lot* of food."

"There's a homeless vet that hangs out in the alley behind our building. I try and bring him some food." I watch him, expecting him to puff out his chest like he's bragging, but instead he grabs a plate and starts scooping food onto it before handing it to me. The man is an enigma.

We eat in companionable silence, probably because we're both stuffing our faces. He's a huge guy, so I'm not surprised that he eats a lot. I really shouldn't eat anymore, though. I've got curves, and if I'm not careful, they'll become more pronounced.

Ryan's hateful words play in my head on a loop: *"I wouldn't need to fuck other women if you weren't a fat fucking pig."* That was usually while I sat watching him cut up the dinner I made, and he'd put my serving on a little plate. Every Monday morning, I would have to step on the scale—if I'd gained, then I got slapped for each pound. God, I was so pathetic and weak.

My eyes burn and my nose tingles. "I-I have to go to the bathroom." Before he can say anything, I bolt toward the restrooms, praying the tears wait until I'm in the privacy of a bathroom stall.

Luckily the room's empty when I step inside, and I quickly shut myself inside the closest stall. I've learned over the years to cry silently—Ryan hated the sound of my crying and could barely tolerate *Grant's* crying. I don't know why I still let him get to me. Sure, it's only been two years, but I got the courage to leave—to press charges in order to protect me and my son.

Of course it was too late for Grant, because he finally witnessed how weak I truly was. "Stop," I whisper to myself. It's not going to do my son any good to see me wallowing in guilt. I take a couple of deep breaths and rapidly blink to stop the tears. Grabbing some toilet paper, I dry my eyes, take a deep breath, and exit the stall.

After splashing some cold water on my face, I head back out to the table to see Erik sticking his card back in his wallet. I sit down across from him.

"How much do I owe you?"

Erik looks up at me, and then his gaze examines my face. I wait for him to ask what's wrong, but instead, he says, "I asked *you* out to lunch. It's on me. I had them box up the food on your plate for you, and the rest is for him."

I nod. "T-Thanks." Picking up my purse, I follow him out of the restaurant and to his car. He doesn't say anything, for which I'm glad. When we pull into the garage and get out of the SUV, I watch Erik grab the bigger container out of the back seat. He's walking to the opening of the garage when a tall, rail-thin man approaches him. The man takes the box and shakes Erik's outstretched hand.

A warm feeling fills me as I watch him with the homeless man. Erik says goodbye to him and leads me toward the elevator. When we reach our floor, he leads me out the elevator with a hand to my lower back like a true gentleman, taking me right to my desk and pulling out my chair for me.

Before I sit, I turn and look up at him. "Thank you for lunch."

He gives me a smile that makes my belly quiver. "You're welcome." Erik takes my container of food. "I'll stick this in the refrigerator for you." I watch him disappear into the back, and then I sit down.

The rest of the day, I work on autopilot. My thoughts are all over the place. Ryan runs through my mind, plus the night I spent with Erik, and then Erik some more every time I see him. By the time five o'clock rolls around, I gather my things and head into the back to grab my food. When I step into the break room, I freeze when I spot Erik with his back to the door, standing in front of the TV.

Erik turns and shoots me a grin. "Taking off?" he asks.

"Yep, but I, ahh...I wanted to ask if you'd like to go get dinner with me." He doesn't say anything, so I quickly add, "Of course it's no problem if you have plans and can't."

He walks closer and stops right in front of me. "I'd love to have dinner with you. How about pizza?"

I nod. Again we head out, and he helps me into the passenger side. We decide to grab pizza at Lou Malnati's. Inside the restaurant, I roll my eyes as every single woman gives Erik googly eyes. We get seated in front of a window that gives us a nice view outside.

Erik orders a beer and I order a glass of wine. My mouth waters when Erik orders us stuffed spinach bread. When they take our pizza order, he requests a large deep-dish pie with sausage. "What are you doing? We can't eat all that."

"I know. I just figure what we don't finish, you can take home to Grant."

I stare at him. Where's the cocky guy who checks out other women in front of me? Where's the cocky grin that seems to always be on his face? "That's really sweet of you." Our waitress drops off our drinks, lingering by our table until I shoot her a look I hope conveys how much I find her unbelievable. I shoot a similar look to Erik when he chuckles.

I stick out my tongue at him, grab my wine, and take a hearty swallow. We make small talk while we wait for our appetizer, and as soon as it comes, we both dig in. Erik takes a swallow of his beer. "What made you decide to ask me out?"

I'm surprised by his question, but a little shocked he didn't ask me sooner. I tear apart the bread in my hand. "I was just hoping we could talk."

CHAPTER SIX

Erik

The waitress takes my card after I argued with Shayla about who was paying. I know she's the one who asked me out, but my mom would throw a fit if I let a woman pay on a date—no matter who made the first move.

When she returns I sign the slip and pick up the box with our leftovers. Shayla takes my hand when I hold it out to her. I don't let go of her as we head outside and to my SUV. Fall is right around the corner, and the evenings are becoming a lot cooler. When we climb in, I turn toward her. "You're so beautiful." I reach out, tucking a loose curl behind her ear.

It's still light enough that I see her cheeks turn the most adorable shade of pink. Her pearly whites bite her lower lip, and I want nothing more than to bite that lip myself. *Fuck*, I'd love nothing more than to sink into her tight pussy again, but she's not ready for that—not yet, at least.

"Thank you." Her voice is soft, but unsure.

"Erik, you don't want to date me. I'm not really in a place where I should be dating, either. Plus you're a good-looking guy, and you can get any woman you want. Not one with the baggage I have."

Something about that statement pisses me off. I take a deep breath. "Your son is *not* baggage. Why do you think that having a child would make you undateable? What kind of guy do you think I am?"

She shrugs. "Most single people want to be able to date and come and go as they please. I have a child, which means I have to arrange for a sitter because his dad isn't in the picture and I don't have any family. It doesn't look good if I'm dumping my kid off to go on dates all the time." Shayla looks away for a moment before turning back to me. "You're right—he's not baggage. My life is just…really complicated."

I want to ask why her son's dad isn't in the picture, but things are delicate with us right now. I'm gonna have to earn her trust before she opens up, and she doesn't seem like someone who trusts easily. Both Carrie and Delilah have little information on her, or at least anything they were going to share.

"What if I *like* complicated? Easy is boring." It hits me that until I met Shayla, I *was* fucking bored. She's kept me on my toes and off my game since I've met her.

We head toward her place, and I'm surprised when she invites me inside. I follow Shayla in. I glance around, and it's small, but quaint. A meow pulls my attention to the couch, where a huge orange tabby cat sits on the arm. Obviously happy his mistress is home, the cat bumps his head into her hand until she bends down and kisses the top of his head.

I reach out to let him smell me, but he turns away from me, giving me the cold shoulder. Shayla laughs softly beside me, and I love that sound. At the office, I'm always catching her laughing with Delilah or one of the guys. I hate it, but not really— *I* just want to be the one who makes her laugh…wait, *what?*

"Have a seat." She signals to the couch. "I'm going to go change real quick."

I watch Shayla disappear down the hall. Instead of sitting, I walk over to some pictures hanging on the wall. A gorgeous little boy with dark hair and dark eyes smiles widely at me from the frame. Moving to the next one, it's Shayla with her boy on her lap. They're not smiling at the camera; they're smiling at each other.

"That's Grant when he was younger," she says from behind me.

Turning, I smile at her. "He's beautiful, like his mom."

"T-Thank you.

I take her in and see that she's in a pair of leggings and an off-the-shoulder t-shirt the color of raspberries. My dick immediately twitches in my jeans, but I will it to go down.

"Do you want something to drink? I don't have much—just water, apple juice, and iced tea."

"I'll take a glass of iced tea. Thanks."

I sit down on Shayla's overstuffed couch and sigh. This thing is like sitting on a firm cloud. I cross my ankle over my knee, and then thank Shayla when she returns with our drinks and hands me mine.

"How long have you worked at Rogue?" she asks.

"About two years. After I left the Marine Corps, I wanted to do something where I still protected people in a way, but didn't want to join the police force. I met Jack when he was just starting his company, and he hired me on the spot. While I got my license as a private investigator, I did some minor surveillance work and helped put together the rest of our team. I've been the head of surveillance for a year now." I take a drink of my iced tea.

"Were you ever deployed?" I know she's just curious, but I honestly don't like talking about it, at least not to people who haven't experienced what I have. Most people don't want to hear about the ugliness we see. Shayla puts a hand on my arm. "I can tell you don't want to talk about it, and that's okay."

I can only nod, because how did she read me— how could she tell I didn't want to talk about it? When I reach out my hand, she takes it and lets me pull her into my side. "Thank you for understanding. It's not always the easiest thing to talk about." I clear my throat. "So, uh, do you need to go get your son?"

She nods. "He's asleep already, but I want to get him into his own bed. Do you want to wait here?"

I stand up. "I'll go with, if you don't mind." After following her out the door, we walk side by side upstairs to the lone door. A beautiful blonde with twists and braids in her hair opens the door, smiling. Shayla hugs her, and that's when the blonde notices me.

"Oh my," she blurts out, causing Shayla to giggle—yes, I said *giggle.*

"Luna, this is Erik. Erik, this is my neighbor/good friend/babysitter, Luna."

I hold my hand out and she takes it excitedly as she looks between the two of us. "It's great to meet you, Erik. Shayla's my girl," Luna says while wrapping her arms around Shayla. It's very clear that the two women really care about each other a lot.

We step inside and I meet Rocco; he's got more of a straight-laced look, but he tells me it's because he's a CPA and works for a nonprofit. The kids are all asleep in the living room—Grant is on the couch sleeping, and Shayla picks him up with practiced ease.

Heading back downstairs, I hold the door open as she walks through with the boy wrapped around her like a spider monkey. I shut, and lock, the door. "I'm going to go put him in bed real quick," Shayla says and then kisses the top of her boy's head.

I can't take my eyes off them together. "Okay, babe." I sit down in the same spot on the couch from earlier.

Shayla comes out a few minutes later. "He's out," she says with a smile as she sits down next to me.

"Your friends seem nice," I tell her honestly. In my line of work, you learn how to read people, and I can tell Luna and Rocco really care about Shayla and her son.

"They're the best. We've been friends since pretty much the day we moved in. They look after Grant, and I look after their girls. Our neighbor downstairs keeps to himself, but he's a nice enough guy."

Shayla turns on the TV, and the Cubs are playing. I hold up my arm, and she scoots over to me, snuggling into my side. We watch the game, talking during the commercial breaks. I'm out of my comfort zone here. By now I'd have already fucked her twice, and would either be gearing up for another round or getting dressed and preparing to make my escape.

I'm not sure how much time passes before I notice Shayla's eyes drooping. I kiss her forehead, and she settles against me. "Come on, lock the door behind me. Get some sleep." We stand up and she walks me to the door. I open it and turn to her. "I had a good time tonight."

"I did too. I still think you could do better than me. I'm a mess." Shayla looks up at me.

Reaching out, I cup her cheek. "I told you earlier, and I meant it. Easy is boring, and lucky for you…" I lean in until our lips are almost touching. "I *like* messy." I kiss her chastely before standing to my full height. "I'm out of the office most of the day tomorrow, but I'll see you in the afternoon."

"O-Okay. Thank you for the leftover pizza. Grant will gobble that up for dinner tomorrow night." She closes the door, and I wait until I can hear the deadbolt click before walking out and heading to my apartment.

***

It's been crazy lately, and we've been so busy that I've really only seen Shayla at the office, but I *have* brought her breakfast or lunch most days. Carrie's back and Shayla is now covering for Delilah, the poor girl.

Fuck me, her own mother had been behind her attack and harassment, and then she *kidnapped* her. Afterward, her and her boy toy induced Delilah—the plan was to deliver her baby and sell it. I've never seen a baby be born before, but when Jack asked for my shirt, I looked down and watched that baby start to slide right out of her momma.

I'll never forget the sound of Delilah's screams as they tore through the night, followed by the sweet cries of little miss Charlotte.

Delilah had some severe emotional issues after the whole ordeal, understandably, but she's doing better now, and is a damn good mom to little Charlotte—or Charlie—who has all of us men wrapped around her teeny, tiny finger.

I get off the elevator and find Carrie behind the front desk. "Hey, beautiful."

She beams at me. "Hey, yourself. How are you, handsome?"

"Living the dream. Gretchen is coming tomorrow to spend the weekend with me." They all know my sister. That's why I love my team—because we're a family and treat each other and our relatives as such.

"If you want, bring her over to see the baby," she says.

"Okay, we may do that." We already have plans to see Charlie. I knock twice on her desk before heading into the back. Shayla is coming down the hall from the break room and greets me with a smile. "Hey, babe."

I hold up a white pastry bag, and she looks at it and then at me. "What's this?"

"I got you one of those chocolate croissants you love, and a cup of fruit." I hand her the bag and she looks inside.

"Thank you, but you don't have to keep buying my meals."

I follow her into her temporary office— Delilah's. "I know I don't, but I want to." I sit down in the chair across from her. "My sister is coming to spend the weekend with me. We're going to go see Delilah and Charlie, and maybe to Navy Pier, or the zoo. Why don't you and Grant come with us?"

She shakes her head. "I don't want to intrude on your time with your sister."

"Trust me, you won't be intruding. My sister loves kids, and she's the neighborhood babysitter. Come on, we'll have a great time."

Shayla sighs. "Okay. That sounds fun."

I don't even bother trying to hide my pleased smile. It's time to start upping my game. I know she's still a little hesitant, but if I can just get past the wall she's got up, then I'm golden. I'm hoping my sister can help. I want her to see I'm so much more than what she saw on our blind date. The connection that I felt is still there, and since we haven't had sex since the first time, it's clear it's not just sexual.

She smiles. "I won't keep you—it's okay, you can go now. Thank you again for breakfast."

I come around Shayla's desk, stopping next to her and squatting down. I'm so much taller than she is that even when I'm squatting I'm still towering over her. Her brown hair is down in loose waves, and I reach out to finger them. I don't miss the way her cheeks turn a deep shade of pink.

"I'll see you later." I lean in, kiss her cheek, and whisper against her ear, "Bye, babe." Inside, I do a fist pump when I feel her do a full-body shiver.

Without another word, I stand up and head out. I find Jack standing in the hall outside his office. "What's up, Grandpa?" The guy smiles widely whenever we talk about his granddaughter. I feel bad, though, because Charlie's never going to be able to date. With Reece for a Dad, Jack for a grandpa, and the rest of us as pseudo-uncles, no man is ever going to hurt her or even get close enough to try.

"Not much. Check out this picture of Charlie smiling." He holds out his phone to me. My sister is really the only kid I've been around, especially as a baby. But Charlie is a beautiful little girl, and in the picture she's sleeping with a tiny smile on her face. "Isn't she just the prettiest baby? Just like her momma."

"She is—she's gorgeous. How's Delilah doing?"

He takes his phone back. "She's better. Since she's nursing, she's using more all-natural remedies for the anxiety. When she comes back, she's going to work from home two days a week and the rest she'll be here. I know a part of her is scared to leave the baby, but Reece's mom is going to come up and help with the transition."

"That's great. Laura's a good woman." Reece's mom reminds me a lot of mine—very maternal, funny, and doesn't put up with any bullshit. I know it was hard on Jack after everything went down with his daughter, especially since it was his ex-wife who was behind it all.

"She is. I'm just glad Del's got a woman in her life like that. How's your family? Is Gretchen finally giving Tad gray hair?"

Shaking my head, I mutter, "I'm already getting them. Do you have a second to talk about the case I'm working on?" I follow him into the office and shut the door.

***

"Is this girl your girlfriend?" Gretchen asks from beside me as we drive across town to Shayla's place.

Gretchen was dropped off by my mom and Tad last night, and then I took them out for dinner at Mom's favorite sushi place. After they left, Gretchen and I went to the movies. Luckily, my sister picks some sort of teen dystopian action movie.

Then for the rest of the night, I had to hear about how hot the actor playing the lead was and how he's the greatest because he does charity work. My sister also shared that she thought his ex was an idiot and he could do better.

By the time she passed out on the couch, I was

ready to smack my head against the wall. Thankfully I still had a bottle of bourbon on top of my refrigerator, and drank two fingers…swiftly.

I love that girl, but she's exhausting. When we got up this morning, we ran to get donuts before we vegged out on the couch and pigged out. I skipped out on my morning run, but it's an easy sacrifice.

Now, we're on our way to pick up Shayla and her son. I'm nervous, and I'm *never* nervous. I want her boy to like me. Shayla and I are so new, and if he doesn't like me, she could easily tell me to take a hike.

I glance at my sister before turning back to the road. "No, she's not." I don't add that I'm not sure what I want. All I know is that I want to at least see if what I want is with her.

After pulling up in front of her place, Gretchen and I hop out as Shayla and her boy come walking toward us. She's carrying his booster seat. "Hey," I say, and she smiles nervously.

My sister goes right up to Grant and squats down in front of him. "Hi, I'm Gretchen. The big guy behind me is my big brother Erik. What's your name?"

He hides behind Shayla's legs. "His name is Grant, or Grunt, which is what I call him." Shayla smiles warmly at my sister. "He'll warm up to you, I promise."

Gretchen gives Grant her biggest, brightest smile. "I think I'll call you Grunt." She takes the booster seat from Shayla and puts it in the back seat before leading Grant to the Explorer and helping him in.

I turn to look at Shayla, and her eyes are wide. "What?" I ask as I walk toward her.

"He's never met her before, and he let her just lead him away—that's insane." She smiles up at me. "She is absolutely gorgeous."

"Thanks." I motion to the SUV. "Shall we?"

Nodding her head, she lets me lead her to the Explorer. I help her inside and then walk around to the driver's side and climb in. I look in the rearview mirror and see that Gretchen is showing Grant something on her phone.

The drive to Reece and Delilah's is uneventful, and Gretchen talks to Grant the whole time. Shayla is turned slightly in her seat, watching the kids in the back with a soft smile on her face. When we pull up in front of the couple's house, I grab the gift that Gretchen brought for the baby out of the back.

Delilah meets us at the door with a huge smile on her face. "Hey, guys." She sees Grant, who is glued to his mom's side. "Oh my gosh! Are you Grunt?" I watch the boy nod his head. "Well, come on in. Charlie can't wait to meet you."

We follow her into the house, and Gretchen grabs the gift she brought for the baby and hands it to Delilah. I have no clue what it is, but Delilah wastes no time opening it. It's an adorable little dress and sandals that are so freaking tiny.

When Reece gets back from what looks like a diaper run, he and I head outside. "She's going to be a beauty," I say. "You look happy." The man looks tired as fuck, but he's smiling.

"I never wanted any of this. I liked being single, but that all changed. I know I sound like a lovesick fool, but fuck me, I *am* one. That baby girl in there and her momma are everything to me." Reece is quiet for a moment before he makes me laugh. "Charlie is *never* going to date."

We talk about work for a little bit before we head back inside. The sight I see when I follow Reece into the living room causes my heart to start pounding. Charlie is in Shayla's arms. My sister is snuggled up next to her with Grant on her lap as they coo over the baby girl.

Shayla looks good with the baby in her arms, and it makes me feel something foreign. I can't tell you what it is because *I* honestly can't even name it. All I know is I want to identify it and explore it. She looks up and shoots me a smile.

I walk farther into the room and notice that Grant is watching Reece and me. His eyes are bright and fearful. That sends me on high alert. Shayla told me that Grant's dad isn't in the picture, but we haven't talked about why. I'm hoping she'll tell me as we get to know each other better.

CHAPTER SEVEN

Shayla

I love Erik's sister. For one, she looks like a real-life Tinkerbell, and she's the sweetest girl I've ever met. She's immediately latched onto my boy, and he's eating it up. I've been able to just sit back and watch him smile, chatter happily, and laugh.

After we left Reece and Delilah's, we took the kids to lunch at Shake Shack, and of course Erik refused to let me pay...*again*. He kept talking to Grant even though my son stayed tucked in between Gretchen and me. The sight made my heart ache and the guilt came roaring back.

Erik would catch the look on my face and reach out, giving my hand a reassuring squeeze. But what would he say if he knew I stayed too long with my abusive ex, and that my son witnessed one of my beatings...what would he say if he knew that's the reason he doesn't like men? Yes, Erik may be hot, and women may fall all over him, but the way he is with his sister warms my heart. You can just tell that he's sweet and loving. Imagining the look of pain on his face when I tell him the truth about my past makes me want to lock everything away. The last thing I want is for him to pity me—I don't want *anyone* to pity me when they hear my story. I want him to see the strength that I had in me to leave.

After lunch, we head down to Navy Pier. I've never been down there since I moved to Chicago, so I'm kind of excited. I know there are some fun things to do for the kids, and I hope that Grant has a good time.

First up we ride the Centennial Wheel; a few older couples ride it with us. I'll admit I'm completely in awe of the view. Grant sits with Gretchen...again, and she points stuff out to him as he asks questions. I sit next to Erik and feel his arm around me.

An older woman with a white-haired pixie cut gives us a blinding smile. "You have a beautiful family," she says. "You should be very proud."

I open my mouth to correct her, but Erik speaks up first. "Thank you. We're *very* proud." He smiles down at me and hugs me into his side. Erik doesn't let go of me until we're stepping out of our cart, or whatever it's called.

Next, the kids and I ride the carousel. Grant isn't tall enough to ride alone, so he and Gretchen ride together. I ride the horse next to them and take a quick picture of them both smiling at me. As we start to go around I look into the small crowd, spotting Erik easily since he's so much taller than everyone else.

Again, when I stand next to Erik, I realize just how large he is. He looks like a giant. A built, blond, gorgeous giant who has the most beautiful dick I've ever seen. Before my husband I only had one other lover—my high school boyfriend. Obviously we didn't know what we were doing, but we learned a lot together. Meanwhile my ex-husband didn't care if I came, or if I was even aroused half the time.

Erik was a giving lover. Sure, it was only one night, but he didn't come unless I did at least twice. I want more of him so bad I can taste it, but I'm scared. I'm scared that the novelty of me will wear off and he'll leave. I'm afraid he'll cheat—I've seen the way women look at him, and hell, on our blind date he checked out the hostess *right* in front of me.

Most of all, I'm afraid that Grant will always be fearful of men, including Erik, and he'd eventually leave us because he couldn't deal with it.

I push all of the thoughts away and give Erik a smile and a wave. When we pass around again, I look at him and shake my head when he gives me a wink. I turn toward the kids, and again I'm smiling—it seems that's all I've done today. My son's smile makes my eyes burn, and my cheeks are aching from smiling so hard.

When the ride stops, I help Gretchen and Grant down from their horse. Erik meets us at the exit and we walk around for a bit. Up ahead is Climbing Walls. I turn to Erik. "Have you done that before?"

"I've done a little climbing. Do you want to give it a try?"

We stop and I look at it, then back at Erik. "Will you do it first?"

He gives me his devastating smile that makes my

77

belly ache. "Yeah baby, I'll do it first." Erik and Gretchen walk ahead of us, and he buys tickets first for him and me.

Erik's sister and Grant walk hand in hand over to the wall, where she says they'll wait for us. He helps me get my harness on, and then I and every other woman there watch him put his on. I follow Erik over to the wall that looks way more advanced than some of the other ones. I move off to the side, watching as he makes his way over to a man standing to the side.

He chalks his hand, and then I watch as he starts climbing. His muscles bulge and contract with each movement. All around me women are stopping to watch him gracefully move up the wall. He's a big man, but fuck me, up there he's *ginormous*.

As I watch him, a tingling starts low in my belly, my breasts feel heavy, and if I close my eyes, I can remember the feel of his lips wrapped around my nipple. *God*, I can still feel his teeth nip at the hardened flesh. At one point he's holding on with just one hand, and his legs are dangling. He's super strong, because the night we had sex he kept picking me up, flipping me around like I weighed nothing.

It suddenly feels very hot, even though it's cool out. I focus back on Erik, and I feel slightly disappointed that he's coming down. When his feet hit the ground, the guy standing there helps unhook Erik and then claps him on the back.

He comes walking toward me looking hot as fuck. I'm guessing that Erik can read the desire on my face because his eyes darken and his tongue peeks out, rubbing back and forth over his lower lip.

When Erik stops right in front of me, a part of me wants him to kiss me—oh hell, it's *all* of me that wants to kiss him. My lips tingle with the memory of his kisses. Every time he did, he dominated my mouth. Of its own volition, my body carries me toward him. "That was amazing," I say with a sigh.

He begins to bend down, his face getting closer to mine, but we both freeze. "Erik, that was awesome," Gretchen calls, skipping over with Grant's hand clasped in hers. Erik wraps his arm around her shoulders.

Grant comes to me and takes my hand. I smile down at my son. "Did you see Erik climb?" My boy nods. "Do you think I should do it?" He looks up at the wall, and then back at me before smiling and nodding. "Okay, stay right next to Gretchen, okay?" He nods again and moves right to Gretchen's side.

"I'll keep him right by me, Shayla." I smile at the girl, and then let Erik lead me over to one of the easier walls.

My palms begin to sweat the closer we get. Once we stop in front of it I look up, and it seems much higher than I originally thought. I'm by no means scared of heights, but my heart begins to race. They hook me up to the safety harness, and I chalk up my hands. I walk up to the base of the wall and take a deep breath.

"You've got this. Just take your time," Erik says from next to me.

I grip the first little handle thingy. Soon I'm making my way up. While I climb, I hear Erik and

Gretchen cheering me on. Then, lo and behold, I hear, "Go Mommy, go!"

I finally reach the top, and then make my way back down. When my feet touch the ground, the attendant unhooks my harness.

Erik grabs me and pulls me into a hug. "You did amazing." I feel his lips on the top of my head and smile when I hear him breathe in deeply. I swear that I hear him growl, too—low and deep in his chest, and it makes me smile. He gives me another squeeze before letting go.

Gretchen climbs the same wall, and then she and Erik race—he's doing the more difficult wall while she does the easy one. Erik, of course, beats his sister with ease. It's no wonder since it would take about three or four of Gretchen to make one Erik.

When we finish, we stop at Ben and Jerry's for ice cream. We eat our cones as we head back to Erik's Explorer and then back toward my place. I turn to Erik. "Thank you for such a fun day." I turn to the back seat. "And it was so nice meeting you, Gretchen."

Gretchen gives me a huge smile. "It was nice meeting you too." Then his sister wraps her arms around Grant. "It was nice meeting you too, Grunt." My boy hugs her back. Erik comes around, and when I get Grant out he grabs my boy's booster seat.

"Bye, Gretchen," my little man says quietly.

Erik smiles at me. "I'm glad you guys had fun today. We did too." He kisses my forehead. "See you Monday."

Grant and I head inside. "Hey buddy, why don't

you take a bath, and then we'll have a movie night."

He nods. "Okay, Mommy." Then he runs down the hall to his room. I watch him run naked into the bathroom and follow him in, turning the water on for him. He splashes around while I sit on the toilet seat reading my Kindle.

When he's turned into a little prune, I wash him up quickly before rinsing him off and pulling him out of the tub. After he's dried off, he's got jammies on, and with his hair combed, we head into the living room followed by Lucifer.

I pop some popcorn while Grunt and Lucifer snuggle into the couch. Our movie extravaganza starts with *Cars* and ends with *Love Actually*—that one's not until my little Grunt falls asleep with his head on my lap. I cry every time Emma Thompson's character opens the box and instead of the necklace, it's the CD. She loses it in the privacy of her bedroom, but then pulls it together.

When the movie ends, I pick up Grant and take him back to his bedroom. I get him settled into bed, and Lucifer jumps up. He curls into the crease of my boy's legs. Bending down, I brush Grant's brown hair away from his forehead and kiss it gently. I take a minute, breathing in his clean little boy scent, and smile.

He snuggles deep into his covers, and then I freeze because it sounds like he mumbled something. "Grant?" I whisper. Sometimes he talks in his sleep. Instead, his little snores fill the bedroom.

I turn on his nightlight before heading back into the living room. My phone dings as I sit down, and when I pick it up, I see a text from Erik.

Erik: I had fun today. My sister called my mom after we got back to my place and told her all about Grant.

I smile as I start typing.

Shayla: I had fun too. Grant fell asleep during our movie marathon.

I watch the black dots dance across the screen, and while I wait for the message to pop up, I grab a handful of popcorn and munch on it.

Erik: Do you guys want to meet us for breakfast tomorrow?

I can't help but smile at the thought of seeing him again. Yes, we see each other at work during the week, but seeing how he is with his sister just further proves that he's a good guy.

Instead of agreeing to meet them for breakfast, I do something that surprises even me.

Shayla: Why don't you guys come here? I make amazing pancakes from scratch. Why don't you come at nine, unless that's too early?

He doesn't even hesitate.

Erik: We'll see you at nine. I'll bring the OJ.

Shayla: Okay, see you tomorrow.

After turning off the living room lights, I head into the bathroom and go through my nightly routine. I smile as I head back into the room while I rub lavender lotion into my arms, but it quickly disappears. I really can't get *too* excited. My complicated life will scare him away in no time.

***

"Erik, would you like another one?" I ask while holding up the skillet with a cooking pancake on it.

They showed up right at nine, and I was pleasantly surprised when Erik held out a bouquet of flowers for me, along with a bag with fruit and orange juice in it. I thanked him and stood on my tiptoes to kiss his cheek. "Thank you."

Again, as soon as they got there, Grant quit talking. He took Gretchen to see his room and while I checked on him, I could hear him talking quietly to her.

Back in the kitchen, I found Erik holding Lucifer. The cat was leaning into him while he scratched behind his ear. "He hates everyone," I told Erik, and he gave me that damn cocky smile of his. "Whatever," I muttered, and then started mixing up the batter.

Erik leaned against the counter right next to me, and together we whipped up chocolate chip pancakes. I called the kids, and they rushed in.

Gretchen smiled at me. "Wow, it smells good in here."

I plated pancakes for both kids, sprinkled sliced strawberries on top, and then finished them off with whipped cream. On Erik's, I just added strawberries, but he gave me a look so I gave him whipped cream too.

Now, I'm scooping up the last pancake and placing it on Erik's plate. After shutting the stove off, I grab a wet paper towel and make quick work of wiping the chocolate from Grant's mouth. "I hope they tasted okay," I say as I grab a grape, popping it into my mouth.

"Babe, they're delicious."

Once we finish, Erik kicks me out of the kitchen, insisting that he would clean up. I read while I sit on the couch, but every time I can hear him clink around in the kitchen, it fills me up with warmth I've never felt before. I push it away when Grunt and Gretchen come into the living room. They lie on the floor and we watch *The Angry Birds Movie*.

When Erik joins us, he sits downs right next to me and wraps his arm around my shoulders. Together, we all sit and watch the movie together, and it feels good.

CHAPTER EIGHT

Shayla

The day has just started and I already want to go home and crawl back into bed. Things started out okay, but then Grant spilled his milk all over himself and my phone; I got it and him cleaned up. Right before I took him up to Luna's, she called and told me Lennon had just thrown up. She tried to apologize for not being able to watch Grant, but I told her it was fine. It's not their fault her baby's sick.

I quickly made Grant snacks and put them in a little lunch bag. He was going to come with me to the office and hang out while I did some work, and then I was going to see about finishing the rest of my tasks from home.

Now we're in our Uber heading toward the office. I hope it's not going to be a problem that Grant is with me. Plus it's an office full of men. But they're my friends and co-workers and I want him to be comfortable with the people I spend time with. He's just finally started warming up to Rocco, and

85

he's a great, standup guy.

I want him to know what it's like to be around good, strong men—not weak woman beaters and deadbeat dads. But let's face it: I'm weak too, because I stayed with the man.

I shake those thoughts off as we get to the office. Thanking the driver, I grab Grant's booster seat and his hand as we head into the building.

Inside the elevator, he looks up at me. "Can I push the button, Mommy?"

"Of course." I show him how to swipe the card, and which button to push. "Good job, honey."

When the doors open, I spot Carrie and Egan standing at the front desk. "Good morning, guys. My babysitter has a sick kiddo, so I brought Grant with me just for a few minutes while I finish a couple of things. Do you think they'll have a problem with him being here?"

Carrie smiles and shakes her head. "Not at all. You know you could've just called me and let me know that you couldn't come in today."

"I know, but I haven't been here very long, and I want to make sure I pull my weight." Plus once Delilah's back, I want to prove my worth so they keep me on.

"I've heard nothing but great things about you. I don't think you'll have to worry too much." Carrie smiles at Grant. "How are you, buddy? Are you going to help your mom work today?"

He smiles and nods at her, but won't look at Egan. I smile at both of them before I head into the back and into Delilah's office. Grant curls up in the chair across from my desk, and I hand him the iPad and headphones. Once he's settled, I log into my computer and go over my to-do list.

Throughout the morning, the men have all learned that Grant is here, so they stick their heads in to say hello to him. Erik brings my son a couple of donuts, and Grant even mumbles a "thank you." Of course, he avoids eye contact the whole time.

When Jack arrives, I step out to talk to him. "Jack, I'm so sorry—I had to bring Grant. I had a couple of things to do, and I didn't want to get behind. Everything else I can do from home." My eyes burn; what if he fires me?

He gives me a soft smile. "Shayla, it's seriously fine. Yes, go work from home. We know how to get ahold of you if we need you." I don't move until he looks pointedly at my office. "Go."

"Thank you, Jack." *God, I hope they keep me on when Delilah comes back.* He nods, and I watch him walk away.

***

I'm typing up my last invoice from my makeshift office at my kitchen table when my phone pings.

Erik: *I just emailed you my billable hours for last week.*

I open my email and click on the one for him. I quickly scan it, and as I'm about to text him back, I see there's a little video icon at the bottom. After clicking on it, I can't help but smile when Erik's gorgeous face appears on my laptop.

"Hey beautiful, I missed seeing you the rest of the day. I hope your day has gone well, and I want you to have dinner with me Saturday night. Please say yes, and I'm not above begging." The video ends with him giving me puppy dog eyes.

Do I want to have dinner with him? Yes, even though I'll have to watch women fall all over themselves to get a look at him while I do. But who am I kidding? I want to have sex with him again too.

I pick up my phone and shoot a quick text to Luna.

Shayla: Hey girl. I hope Lennon is feeling better. I have a proposition for you: If Lennon's feeling better, how about Friday night the girls stay with me, and maybe Saturday Grunt could stay with you?

The black dots immediately start dancing.

Luna: YEEEESSSSSSSSSSSSSSSSSSSS!!!!!!!! Momma needs some adult time. The girls would love to have a sleepover. Us keeping Grant, does this mean that you have a date?

Shayla: Yeah, Erik wants to have dinner.

Luna: OMG!! Tell him yes, right now. We'll keep Grant all night!!! Oh and Len is feeling better. She never had a fever, and only threw up twice. Hopefully it's not a bug that's going around.

I smile because that is so Luna: spazzy, sweet, and the world's biggest cheerleader.

Shayla: Thanks girl! If you need me to help with anything just text me, or come down.

Turning back to my laptop, I hit reply and start typing.

Erik,
Yes, I'd love to have dinner with you Saturday night.
Shayla.

He answers me almost instantly, and I can't help but laugh.

Shayla,
That makes me incredibly happy. Make sure you pack an overnight bag, because I'm not letting you go until I've had my fill of you.
Your slave,
Erik

Grant comes running into the kitchen. "Mommy, I'm hungry."

"Okay, baby. I'll make dinner pretty soon. Why don't you grab a banana right now?" He grabs one and then runs back into the living room.

I send Carrie an email letting her know that I'm

signing off, but that I'll be in tomorrow. Plus I'll be covering the front desk while she takes Leif to his well-baby check. Once I shut down my laptop, I make Grant and me some dinner and read him some stories.

CHAPTER NINE

Erik

Looking at the clock, I see that Shayla should be here in about a half hour. After she agreed to come for dinner earlier in the week, I've been like a kid waiting for Christmas morning to come. I made sure to stop in the office every day to see her. I brought her breakfast, lunch, or other little snacks, and I know that sounds like I'm trying to buy her affection, but I'm not. If anything, I'm trying to woo her.

I know she's reluctant to do anything with me and that I intimidate her. I didn't make a good impression on our first date, but I guess I've always been a natural flirt. To be completely honest, I haven't "dated" since high school, and even then it was just about getting my dick wet. Now don't get me wrong, I've never treated women badly, but I didn't want to get serious...*ever*. It was easier to be superficial and selfish and only seek out the women who acted the same way. Then they never got too close—then they never *wanted* to.

My mom thinks it's because I watched her drown in grief when my father was killed—maybe it is, and because of that I've shied away from serious relationships. Either way, I've just never had the desire to settle down. Of course I'm not thinking about settling down with Shayla, but I'm drawn to her.

I know she's drawn to me too, and we owe it to ourselves to see if there's anything there—sexual or emotional. She's got a child—a small child that doesn't seem to like me much, but from what the other guys in the office said he didn't really talk to them either. They said he seemed skittish.

Today I've cleaned my apartment from top to bottom. I got my mom's recipe for baked ziti and then went to the store. Besides those ingredients, I also got garlic bread, salad, and then cheesecake for dessert. If I have it my way, I'll be eating the cheesecake off Shayla's naked body tonight.

In my bedroom, I check the nightstand and see the unopened box of condoms I bought—Magnum, of course. I change the sheets on my bed—not because I've fucked anyone in it, because I don't bring women here—but because she's staying all night and I want her to be comfortable. I even stocked some bath bombs, hoping that I can get her to soak in my Jacuzzi tub with me.

When I head back into the living room, I take a big whiff—the ziti smells amazing. The garlic bread is wrapped in foil, and the salad is tossed. I wanted to pick up her up, but she adamantly refused to let me.

My thoughts are interrupted when the buzzer

sounds, signaling that Shayla is here. I press the button to unlock the door downstairs, then open my front door just as I hear the elevator ding. The moment she steps off I want to swallow my tongue. She's in jeans that are molded to her shapely legs. Her top is a fitted blue t-shirt that showcases her beautiful tits and hourglass figure.

Her brown hair is down in sleek strands, and her makeup is light. She walks slowly toward me, looking unsure—probably because I'm staring at her like a creeper. Shayla stops right in front of me. "Hey." Her voice is soft.

"Hi. Come in." I want to maul her right now, but instead, when she steps inside I kiss her softly on the cheek. "Let me give you the tour, and I'll take this." I grab her bag, and we first walk into the living room.

"I've tried to make it look more domesticated in here for my sister. But they would've revoked my man card if I didn't get a huge flat-screen, and that's the only reason why I have it." I give her a cheeky grin.

"Yes, I'm sure they would've taken it and kicked you right out." She walks over to the sliding door that leads out to my little balcony. "Wow, this view is incredible." I step behind her and take it all in.

"Thanks. That's why I rented this place. Sometimes when I've had a shitty day, I'll sit outside, drink a beer, and just chill. Come on, let's finish the tour." I show her Gretchen's room.

"You did this for her?"

I nod. "Yeah, I wanted her to feel comfortable when she's here." She steps in and looks around.

Gretchen's daybed is against the far wall and covered in a shitload of lavender, from the pillows to the fucking dust ruffle. A white desk sits in front of the window, covered with pictures.

Shayla walks over to it and picks up a picture frame. I move until I'm standing with my front snug to her back, and rest my hands on her shoulders. "That was her second birthday." Gretchen is sitting on my shoulders in her little purple dress, and her cake-covered hands were gripping my hair. "She got the icing in my ears."

Shayla looks up at me and smiles widely. "That is the sweetest picture I've ever seen. I can tell how much she loves you, and you love her. How old were you here?"

"Eighteen, and she was my shadow. It killed me when I left for boot camp, and I hated being away from her. My mom says it was hard on Gretch too." The night I left flies through my mind. My sister wouldn't leave my side and cried her little heart out when it was time for her to go to bed.

I picked her up to hug her, and then she screamed and clung to me until *I* started to cry. I ended up sleeping in her bed with her clinging to me.

Shayla puts a hand to her heart. "Awww…that breaks my heart for you guys." She puts the picture down and picks up the one of me in my dress blues where Gretchen is standing next to me with her arms around my waist. "You were very handsome in your uniform."

I won't tell her that I tagged a lot of ass because of that uniform. "Thanks, babe." She sets the picture down and follows me out of the bedroom. I show her the hallway bathroom, and then lead her to my bedroom. Again she glances around and sees my king-size bed, which is covered in the softest, most expensive sheets I've ever bought. They're the color of eggplant and buttery soft as soon as you slide under them; the duvet cover is a dove gray that my mom bought for me.

The bed sits on a platform made of wood painted a darker gray. My chest of drawers and dresser are both the same color. In the corner of the room sits a tall full-length mirror. The thought of fucking Shayla from behind as I watch us in its reflection makes my dick twitch.

I set her bag on the floor in front of my closet. In the en suite, I show her the glass shower and the huge tub. "I'm hoping to get you in that, later." Shayla's body does a full shudder; I bury my face in her neck and kiss her delicate skin.

Before I can do anything else, the timer calls out from the kitchen. She follows me out and I have her sit at the kitchen table. I pull the ziti from the oven and it looks delicious. Quickly, I toss the garlic bread into the oven before pulling out the salad.

When I'm finally sitting down, we're quiet as we fill our plates. I love that she's not shy and takes a healthy portion of the ziti and a big piece of garlic bread. Shayla moans around each bite of the ziti and my dick is trying to punch a hole through my denim.

She catches me staring, and her cheeks turn a deep shade of pink. "Sorry, it's really, *really* good."

"Don't apologize. I'm glad you're enjoying the

food. I'd love to take credit for the recipe, but it's my mom's." I take a huge bite of my garlic bread, and even I can't help but moan around the wad in my mouth. "Fuck, this *is* amazing."

After we eat, she insists on cleaning up. I compromise and side by side we get the leftovers packaged up, the counters wiped down, and the dishwasher loaded and running. She grabs herself another glass of wine, and I grab myself a beer.

In the living room, we sit together on the couch and watch *John Wick: Chapter Two*. I was surprised when she suggested it, but it's entertaining, and we're both into it. By the time the movie is over, I've got Shayla on my lap snuggled against me.

What happens next surprises the fuck out of me. She pushes against my chest until she's swinging one leg over, straddling me. I don't move and let her do whatever it is that she wants to do to me. She can't miss my erection that she's sitting snuggly on. My hips want to thrust up, but I use my self-control and hold myself *very* still.

Shayla grabs my face and slowly lowers her mouth to mine. She begins kissing me with a gentle glide of her lips. As she begins to deepen the kiss, she begins to move against me. I almost forgot how good of a kisser she is. Shayla licks the seam of my lips and continues to rock against me.

I open my mouth to her, and our tongues dance. Her unique flavor explodes on my tongue, and then I can't hold back any longer. I cradle the back of her head, holding her hair in a tight grip, and then take control of the kiss. She whimpers into my mouth. I let go of her hair and then find the hem of her shirt.

When I slide my hands under the material, I find her skin is warm and soft.

I feel her nipples harden when I cup her breasts through her bra. I pinch them, and Shayla's back arches as she cries out. After pulling her shirt up and off I bend down, wrapping my lips around the hardened bud through the silky material. She whimpers as I nip it with my teeth. I pull down the cups of her bra and moan. Her nipples are so pink and hard. My tongue swirls around and around, then I suck it into my mouth and suckle while she grips my hair.

"Oh yes, just like that," she moans, rocking harder against my dick. I need to be inside her—like *now*.

"Hold on to me, baby." She lets out a squeal but clings to me like a spider monkey.

Carrying her into my room, I climb onto my bed and then lay her down. Fuck me, she's beautiful spread out on my bed. Her hair fans out across my pillow. I peel off my t-shirt, and then pull her bra off before attacking her lips again. This time it's a wild gnashing of lips, tongues, and teeth. I feel her legs wrap around my hips.

Her breasts rub against my chest as I roll my hips, rubbing my aching cock again her jeans-covered pussy. The desire to taste her overpowers me, and I begin my descent down her body. I grab both of her tits, pushing them together before sucking one into my mouth, then the other. When I nip both nipples, she cries out and it's like music to my ears.

I kiss down her slightly rounded belly as I

unbutton her jeans. As I work her jeans and panties off, I inhale the scent of her arousal and my dick gets even harder. Once she's naked from the waist down, I stand up and shuck my jeans off. I'm going commando, so there are no boxers to take off.

I get on the end of the bed on my knees and stare down at her. She's a wet dream, and I can't wait to stick my cock inside her. "Spread your legs and show me your pussy. I want to see how wet you are."

Shayla bites her lip, and I wait with bated breath to see what she's going to do. After what feels like forever, she bends her knees and spreads her legs. My mouth waters as I look at her very wet, pink folds. I move closer, grabbing the backs of both of her thighs. I push them back to give me a better view.

"First, I'm going to eat your pussy until you come, and then I'm going to fuck you so hard."

I lie on my stomach and lean forward, taking one long swipe over her cunt. Immediately I moan as her flavor explodes on my tongue. With each pass of my tongue, she gets more and more wet. Her cries make me feast on her more. I use my thumbs to open her more and more to me, and begin to fuck her with my tongue.

I rub her throbbing clit, and then thrust two fingers inside of her. That's all it takes before she cries out, her channel tightening on my fingers and trying to suck them deeper into her body. She's so fucking wet her body makes squelching sounds as I slowly pump my fingers in and out of her.

When the ripples finally stop, I pull them from

her body, and while she watches, I lick her cum from my fingers. I move until I'm hovering above her—if I would just lower my hips, my dick would be right at her entrance. Instead, I take a finger that's covered in her juices and paint her lips with it.

A groan slips past my lips as she sucks the digit into her mouth. I need to kiss her, so I pull the digit from her mouth and, in an easy glide, begin to kiss her like my life depends on it. She wraps one hand around my shoulder and the other around my dick. Slowly, she pumps it up and down.

My balls begin to tingle, so I pull back slightly. "Are you ready to get fucked?"

"Yes, please." She licks at my lips, and I blindly reach out, grabbing the box of condoms. Shayla takes the box from me and quickly opens it, taking one foil packet out and then ripping it open.

With deft fingers, she slides the condom on then helps guide me to her opening. The crown of my cock is resting just inside of her. She's so hot, and so wet, but before I begin pushing inside of her, I grab her arms. I shackle both wrists with one hand—it puts her breasts in the perfect position for me to give her nipples a quick suck before thrusting inside her until my balls rest against her ass.

She cries out as her pussy spasms around my thick length, and it's music to my ears. "Fuck, baby. You're so tight, and you feel like heaven."

Once I know she's adjusted to my length, I pull almost all the way out before thrusting back inside. I let go of her wrists and she grips my shoulders as I roll my hips, driving my dick deeper inside of her.

Grabbing her thighs, I open her further to my punishing thrusts.

"Do you like that, baby?" I let go of one of her thighs and grab onto the headboard. With each thrust I hit her clit and feel her walls clench around me.

"Oh God, *yes*. Fuck me hard," she moans.

I get up on my knees and wrap her legs around my waist before pulling her up so we're chest to chest. I begin bouncing her up and down on my cock. "Kiss me," I groan, and she obliges me. Of course our kiss is just moaning into each other's mouths. "Are you going to come like a good girl?"

"Yes…You feel so good inside me. *Oh shit*!" She begins to come violently; her body shakes and shudders and I can feel her juices wetting my groin. While she's still coming, I put her on her back and begin pounding into her so violently that I should be concerned that I'm hurting her.

When I begin to come, I bury my face in her neck, groaning as my cum fills the condom. My breathing slows, and Shayla rubs her hands up and down my back. She whimpers as I pull my softening cock out of her.

Shayla gives me a dopey grin, and I lean down to kiss her lips. "Let me get rid of this. I'll be right back."

I climb out of bed and head into the en suite to get rid of the rubber, use the toilet, and wash my hands. Back in the bedroom, I find Shayla right where I left her. Why does she look so right in my bed? I shake the thought off and climb in beside her. I situate us so that we're both under the covers and she's practically lying on top of me, and I like it.

"Get some rest, sweetheart—I haven't even begun to get my fill yet."

CHAPTER TEN

Shayla

My eyes flutter open, and I roll over finding Erik's side of the bed empty. The scent of bacon wafts in through the open bedroom door, and my stomach immediately growls. Throwing back the covers, I moan as I sit up. My muscles ache, and I swear my vagina hurts.

I've never had that much sex in one night. After the first time, we lay there for about ten minutes before my hand began to wander. His dick was hard before I even reached it. Before I had time to think about it, he'd flipped me so I was on top of him with my face hovering over his dick. I grabbed it at the base and licked the purple crown.

I moaned around it as I felt him lick my pussy. I should've been embarrassed by the position we were in, but instead I began to suck his dick harder, and faster. He moaned against me, and I felt it all the way to my clit. It didn't last long because again he flipped us around until I was straddling him. He quickly sheathed himself and then lowered me onto his cock.

Riding him while he sucked my nipples brought me to orgasm so fast that I couldn't even make a sound, but I know Erik felt it when I came because he groaned against my breasts. "Jesus, you're squeezing the fuck out of my dick, baby. You're soaking me." He followed me and grabbed my hips, holding me firmly down on him.

That's how it went until about five in the morning when we both finally passed out.

Gingerly I climb out of bed, grab his shirt off the floor, and pad into his bathroom. After using the toilet, I wash my hands and brush my teeth. I make my way into the kitchen and find Erik at the stove in a pair of flannel pants that sit low on his hips.

God he's big, I think to myself. He turns around and gives me a smile so sweet that it makes my heart flutter in my chest. Erik holds his hand out to me, and I don't even think twice. I place my small hand in his large one. He pulls me close and kisses my lips gently. "Good morning, baby. How'd you sleep?"

"Good, when I slept." I get up on my tiptoes and press another kiss to his chin. "But it was worth it."

He plates our breakfast: scrambled eggs, bacon, and buttered toast. As I dig in, Erik places a hand on my arm. "What time do you have to be back to Grant?"

"Probably by noon." I want to spend some time with him before the new week starts.

He nods. "I'll take you home when you're ready."

We clean up after breakfast and then soak in his

big tub together. He knows I'm sore, so all we do is kiss, and he uses his fingers on me until I come. I didn't really think it was possible to come this much, but he's proving me wrong.

Once we're out of the tub we get dressed—him in jeans and a t-shirt that molds to his body, and me in leggings and an off-the-shoulder sweatshirt. I pack my things in my bag, and before I can sling it over my shoulder, Erik grabs it then grabs my hand and walks me out to the living room.

He slips on tennis shoes, and I honestly don't think I've ever seen him in them before. Hand in hand, we head out. The music playing from his radio is the only sound that can be heard as we make our way toward my place.

When we pull up, there's a spot in front of my building. Erik throws the car into park and turns toward me. "I don't want to leave you yet, but I know you're wanting to spend time with your boy."

I know I should thank him for last night, get out of his SUV, and go get my boy, but something tells me I should invite him to spend time with us. The more positive male role models in Grant's life, the better. "Would you like to hang out with us today? We're probably just going to watch movies and maybe order some takeout."

He smiles widely at me. "I'd love to hang out with you guys."

We get out and make our way to my door. I let us into my place, praying that it's not a total pigsty. Lucifer greets us at the door and winds his way around Erik's legs. I take my bag into my bedroom and leave it on my bed.

Back in the living room, I find Erik sitting in the corner of the couch with Lucifer next to him. "I'll be right back—I'm going to go get Grant."

"I'll wait right here, babe." He nods, and I make my way up to Luna and Rocco's place.

Before I even knock, Luna is opening the door wearing the biggest smile on her face. She grabs my arm, pulling me into her apartment. "I need details," she whispers.

My cheeks heat up just thinking about last night. "It was great." Luna does this twirly little dance, and it makes me laugh. "*Stop*—I don't know what's going to happen, but he's downstairs and is going to hang out with us."

She looks at me wide-eyed. "*Really?* That's great."

"I don't know. We'll see how it goes. I'm sure if he knew about Ryan then he'd run the other way."

"He doesn't seem like the type to run. It'll be good for both you and Grant—he can see his mom spend time with a man that treats her well, because he does, doesn't he?"

"Of course he does, but maybe it's too soon for him to be around Grant." I start to doubt my decision.

"It's not too soon. Maybe for a while just let him think Erik's just your friend. I mean, look how long it took Grant to warm up to Rocco, and even now he only talks to him when he has to." She rests her hands on my shoulders. "I just want you to have some fun and a little bit of the happiness that you make sure everyone else has."

I wrap my arms around her, hugging her tight.

"Thank you."

We head into the girls' bedroom and find them all sitting on Lennon's bed and watching something on the iPad. They look up when we walk in. "Hi, Mommy."

"Hey Grunt, can you give the girls hugs?" He gets off the bed and then hugs Starr and Lennon. Grant hugs Luna and gives her a kiss on the cheek. "We'll see you tomorrow," I tell her, leading him back to our apartment.

When we reach our door, I squat down in front of my son. "Do you remember Erik? He and his sister, Gretchen, hung out with us." Grant nods. "Well, he's come over to hang out with us today. I thought maybe we could watch movies, and then maybe order Chinese later. Does that sound good?"

He reluctantly nods. When we step through the door, Erik stands up. "Hey, Grant. How are you?"

My son looks up at Erik and shrugs his shoulders. Before I can stop Grant, he runs down the hall to his room.

I look up at Erik. "Sorry."

"It's okay. Don't apologize—I know he needs to be comfortable around me at his own speed." See, there's so much more to him than the cocky man I first met.

The first movie we watch is *The Incredibles*, and Erik seems to really enjoy it, but I'm not surprised because it *is* pretty awesome. Grant lies on the living room floor with Lucifer cuddled against him. When Erik gets up to use the bathroom, Grant watches him like a hawk, not relaxing until he sits back down.

106

It makes my stomach turn to watch that happen, and hopefully Erik doesn't notice. After he situates me in the crook of his arm, we decide to watch *Cars 2*. Shortly after it starts, I fall asleep with my head on Erik's shoulder.

I don't know how long I fell asleep for, but I wake up to the sound of Erik talking. "Do you want to wake your mom up, and then we'll order some grub?"

Holding really still, I feel Grunt's little fingers poking my nose. That's how I wake him up most days. I surprise him by wrapping my arms around him and tickling his sides while he giggles. It's one of the most beautiful sounds I've ever heard. For a long time he barely talked and I was afraid he'd be traumatized forever.

Erik helps me sit up, and I see they're watching *Cars 3* now. "Sorry, I didn't mean to fall asleep."

He leans in, whispering in my ear. "I'm not surprised you fell asleep. I didn't let you sleep much last night." His breath hits me, causing goosebumps to break out all over my skin.

"Stop, you're terrible," I whisper back.

I order us some Chinese food. Erik insists on paying and won't take no for an answer. He goes as far as to threaten to call them back if I tried to give them my debit card number. Instead he hands me his card and stands right in front of me until I give the person on the other end of the phone the numbers.

"You're a pain in the butt," I tell him.

He shrugs his massive shoulders. "Yeah, but you still like me."

107

It's true—I do like him, even though a small part of me tells me to run. That he's going to hurt me— not like how Ryan hurt me, but Erik's the type of guy that if I let him too close, he could destroy my heart.

When the food arrives, Erik helps me set it up on the kitchen table. It's safe to say that we're all silent because we're stuffing our faces. When we finish, I clean up while Erik and Grant go to the living room and start playing with Grant's remote control cars. It makes me smile to hear them zipping around on the floor.

Peeking in on them, I smile. Sure, they're playing together, but my son avoids getting close or talking to Erik. The giant blond man smiles as his car chases Grant's around the room. Lucifer sits on the arm of the couch watching the whole thing, looking bored as usual.

It's seven o'clock when Erik stands up to leave. Grant is reading a book in his room, waiting for me so he can have his bath.

At the door, Erik grabs my hand. "I had a really good time." He reaches out, tucking some of my hair behind my ear. "Thank you for letting me get to know your boy a little bit more tonight."

"We had a good time too. I'll see you tomorrow?" Sometimes he's out of the office a lot, but if he's there, he usually stops and says hi to me.

"I won't be in until after lunch, but I'll pop in when I get there." Erik leans down and kisses me softly on the lips. "Bye, baby." I watch him walk down to his SUV and then drive away.

"What am I doing?" I whisper before shutting

108

my door.

***

It's been two weeks since Erik and I spent the night together. He's been working a lot lately—a huge case that he and Marcus are working on has monopolized a lot of his time. I miss him, and the fact that I do scares the crap out of me. When he's out of town he texts me, checking in, and never hesitates to ask about Grant, which I love.

Thanksgiving is the day after tomorrow, and honestly, I hate the holidays. My parents haven't spoken to me in a long time; Ryan made sure to sever those relationships. It hurts that, even though I reached out after I left him, they still refused to speak to me.

I have an older brother, Jim, and he's cut me off as well. He's married and has two little ones that I've never met.

Luna, Rocco, and the girls usually head down to Springfield, where their families live. Everyone else has plans, so Grant and I will spend the day alone, watching the parade and then eating turkey and all the fixings.

I could invite Erik over, but I'm sure he'll go see his own family. When Carrie and Delilah have asked me about my plans, I've changed the subject, and hopefully they haven't realized what I'm doing.

Jack, being the incredible boss that he is, is closing down the office starting Wednesday at noon, and it won't be open again until Monday. It's gotten really cold the past couple of weeks, and soon there will be snow on the ground.

I'm getting ready to work on bills when there's a knock at my door. I smile when Erik pokes his head in. "Hey babe, you got a second?"

"Sure, come on in."

He comes in, shuts the door, and walks around my desk. Erik holds his hand out to me and pulls me up. His lips are on mine immediately, and I automatically open to him. Our tongues duel, and I grab onto the sides of the shirt he's wearing. When he finally pulls back, he uses his thumb to wipe my lip gloss, which I'm sure is smeared now. "I missed you," he says quietly.

That's the first time he's ever said that to me, and it warms a spot deep inside me. "I've missed you too."

"Marcus finally caught the skip."

"That's great. You guys have worked hard to find him."

He hugs me to his chest, and I inhale the woodsy scent that is unique to him. "Yeah, I'm taking tomorrow off and heading to see my family for Thanksgiving. What plans do you have for the holiday?"

Time to show off my superb acting skills. "Oh, you know…a little of this, a little of that."

"Do you have family that you're going to spend time with?" His gaze is like a laser beam, and I fight to keep my gaze neutral.

"Umm…no, it'll just be a quiet day." See, it's a noncommittal answer. I give him a smile. "I really should get these bills done."

"Okay, I'll talk to you later." Erik bends down,

touching his lips to mine before disappearing out of my office.

***

It's Thanksgiving morning, and Grant is waiting patiently for me to finish making the chocolate chip waffles he requested. Once we sit down to eat, I'm elbow deep in whipped cream when there's a knock on the door. My heart starts to race a little, and I don't know why. It's just that Luna and Rocco left town yesterday. Erik was heading to his parents' house yesterday after work, and everyone else is gone.

Maybe a teeny tiny part of me always tries to be prepared for the day that Ryan decides to come back into our lives and wreak havoc. As I walk toward the door, I chastise myself for having such thoughts. It's been two years, and there's been nothing. I know he's out of jail, so that's not it.

When I peek through the peephole, I'm shocked by what—I mean who—I see. I unlock the door with a smile on my face. "Erik? What are you guys doing here?" Erik and Gretchen are at our door.

"We wanted to see if you and Grant wanted to have Thanksgiving with us. I should've called, but we wanted to surprise you. What do you say?" They give me hopeful smiles. They may not look alike otherwise, but they both have the same smile.

"Um…well, I don't want to impose." I shift from foot to foot.

"It's not an imposition at all. My mom sent us to come get you."

"We both have to get ready," I tell them. "Do I have time to take a quick shower?"

Erik nods. "Of course. We're not eating until three."

I step back from the door and they both walk in. Grant comes running into the living room, and his eyes light up when he spots Gretchen. She opens her arms. "There's my buddy!" My sweet boy runs right to her, hugging her tight.

"I'll get his clothes out and lay them on his bed. Gretchen, if you could have him get dressed, that'd be awesome." The tiny blonde smiles and nods. "Thanks, sweetheart."

Erik follows me back to Grant's bedroom, looking sexy as he leans against the door frame. "I'm sorry if I put you on the spot, just showing up like this."

I stand right in front of him. "It's okay, seriously. Are you sure that it's okay that we come? I don't have anything for us to bring."

"My mom said to just bring yourselves."

After I get Grant's clothes laid out I hurry to grab mine, pull my hair up, and jump in the shower. I make it a quick one and hurry through the process of putting some makeup on. I brush out my hair and then put it into a cute knot on top of my head. I throw on some maroon leggings and a black sweater that is flattering to my curvy figure.

I hurry to my bedroom and grab my black riding boots, sliding them on. In the mirror, I look myself over and then head out into the living room. "Does this look okay?"

"Shayla, you look hot!" That comes from

Gretchen.

"Thanks sweetie, and thank you for getting Grant ready." My boy is wearing boot-cut jeans and a long-sleeved red t-shirt.

I quickly clean up the kitchen from breakfast, and then the four of us head out.

It's an hour-and-a-half drive, but I love watching the scenery pass by. It's kind of funny that we're both from Wisconsin and ended up in Chicago.

Gretchen and Grant watch something on her phone. They both have an earbud in one ear, and when I look at Erik, I see that he's wearing a smile. I grab my phone and use my stealth skills to take a quick picture of them. I look at it before quickly showing it to him. "Send that to me," he says.

I do as he says and then just watch the passing scenery, feeling content for the first time in a long time. A chill creeps up my spine, though—I look in the rearview mirror and don't see anyone. Ugh, I need to get a grip.

A while later, we pull up in front of a beautiful Craftsman-style home. The siding is a grayish-blue, the trim is white, and around the base is brick. On the huge porch are a couple of wicker chairs and a little table between them. My hands tremble as we climb out and make our way up to the door.

Erik pushes the front door open and calls out for his mom. A petite blonde woman comes out, wearing a huge smile on her face. "Hello! You must be Shayla and Grant. I'm Erik's mom, Nicole." Instead of shaking my hand, the woman wraps her arms around me in a hug that makes me feel so welcome.

"It's nice to meet you too." I reach for Grant's hand. "Grant, this is Gretchen and Erik's mom. Can you say hello?"

He doesn't speak—he just waves at her. Gretchen comes forward. "Come on, Grant. Let's go see if the parade is on."

Little Tinkerbell takes Grant's hand and leads him farther into the house. I look at Nicole. "He is absolutely smitten with your daughter."

Nicole loops her arm through mine and leads me farther into the house as well. "She's always been really good with kids. Gretchen may only be fourteen, but she knows that whatever she does as a career, it has to deal with children."

"She's got a gift," I tell her.

CHAPTER ELEVEN

Erik

Tad, his brothers, and I are watching football in the family room. It's been a fantastic day. Shayla has gotten along with everyone and seems like she's having a good time. After we went and picked them up, Shayla hung out in the kitchen with my mom and Aunt Peg, drinking wine and carrying on like a bunch of school girls—giggling and whispering about God knows what.

I've never brought a girl home before, but the thought of Shayla and Grant spending the day alone didn't sit right with me. As soon as I mentioned it last night to my mom, she immediately suggested that we go get them and bring them over.

Grant stayed by Gretchen's side the whole time and got really quiet being around the guys. I noticed he was very watchful too—it was like he was waiting for something to happen. When Shayla had spent the night I'd wanted to ask her about Grant's dad, but there had never seemed to be a right time.

I have the means at the office to check into her

past, but I don't want to betray her trust. The more she grows to trust me, the more likely she'll be to tell me about her past on her own…hopefully. Tad and his brother Jeff pulled me outside earlier to grill me.

"She's beautiful, but not the type of girl I've seen you with," Tad said. I've never brought girls home, but my parents would sometimes see me out with girls when I was younger. And yeah, they were all the same: tall, leggy, and blonde with big boobs.

"Yeah, I know. She's got a mouth on her too. On our first date the waitress hit on me, and I thought Shayla was going to whoop her butt." Tad's a very laid-back pastor, but I do try to watch my mouth around him.

"Good, you need someone who keeps you on your toes. You're a good-looking guy and have probably had it easy with every other woman…but easy is boring."

I shake my head, because he's right. She *hasn't* been easy, and even though she's softened to me a little bit, there's still a wall around her.

Now we've just finished eating dessert and everyone is lounging around the family room watching a movie. Shayla's snuggled up next to me on the love seat, Gretchen and Grant are lying on the floor in front of the fireplace, and the rest of the adults are sprawled out on the couch and recliners.

Dinner was just us and the aunts and uncles, but people have been stopping by on and off all day. Women from the church love bringing my family food, and I know it irritates my mom. Tad's a good-looking guy, and even though he's married, some of the female parishioners still come "visit" him. My mom, ever the welcoming host, deals with it.

An hour into the movie, I feel Shayla go slack against me. "Erik, why don't they just spend the night?" my mom says. "Grant can sleep on the futon in Gretchen's room, and Shayla can sleep with you." It *has* been a long day, and to be honest I wasn't looking forward to the long drive back to their place.

I nod in gratitude. "Thanks."

When the movie's over, I gently wake Shayla and tell her the plan. She, of course, declines at first until my mom goes in for the kill. "Sweetheart, it's late and really cold out. We have the room and would love to have you. Please stay."

"Y-Yes, okay. Thanks."

My mom and sister lead Shayla and Grant toward my sister's room, and I get up off the love seat. Tad and his brother are both staring at me. "What?"

"I never thought I'd see the day when a woman stole your heart." Tad follows me into the kitchen, where I grab myself, Tad, and Jeff a beer.

I lean against the counter, taking a swig. Both men look at me expectantly. "It's still new, but I want to see where it goes."

"She's great, son," Tad says with a smile on his face. "That Grant sure is smitten with your sister."

"Very true. They seemed to have fun today. I felt bad ambushing her this morning, but I knew if I called she'd make excuses for why she wasn't gonna be able to come. Plus she knows how much Grant likes Gretchen."

We finish our beers and all head to bed. Before I head to my room, I peek in on my sister and Grant. They're both already in snoozeville—Grant is curled into a ball on the futon, and Gretchen is buried under a mound of blankets.

The master bedroom is on the opposite side of Gretchen's room. Luckily mine is in the basement, for privacy. Shayla comes out of the hallway bathroom. "Hi," she says quietly.

"I peeked in on Grant, and he's already asleep."

She snuggles into my side. "Thanks for checking on him."

I lead her down to my old room. The walls are no longer covered in Green Bay Packers and Victoria's Secret model posters. Now it's just my bed but with a flower comforter on it, and empty dressers that used to be filled with my clothes. No one stores things in here; it's empty except if I stay for an extended period.

Shayla looks around in disbelief. "This is *your* room?"

"Yeah, I know. The posters came down the minute I shipped out for boot camp. Now it's a 'guest room' unless I'm home."

She climbs under the covers and then pulls her leggings off, dropping them next to the bed.

"Seriously?"

Shayla shrugged. "This is your parents' house."

"They have you sleeping down here with me—I think they know we've had sex." I pull off my t-shirt and take my jeans off before climbing into bed. After turning the bedside lamp off, I pull her into my arms. "Now shut up and cuddle me."

118

She slaps me in the stomach, and I tickle her sides until she squeals. "You're a real buttface." In all my life, no one has ever called me that. Shayla gets quiet for a moment. "Thank you for inviting us to spend the day with you. Grant's the only family I have, and sometimes it's lonely to spend the holiday not surrounded by family or friends."

This is the most she's opened up to me—maybe it's because it's dark and we can't see each other. "You're welcome. They enjoyed having you both here today."

It isn't long before her body goes limp and her soft snores fill the room. I take a moment to just savor the feel of her in my arms, and not long after, I let sleep pull me under.

***

A moan slips past my lips. My eyes open, and that's when I realize that Shayla's mouth is wrapped around my cock. "*Fuck*, baby, that's good." She moans around my length and swallows me down as deep as she can go before swirling her tongue around the crown of my cock. I let her get a few sucks in before I pull her off and hoist her up my body.

"I'm sorry," she whispers. "I know this is your parents' house, but it was hard and poking me in the stomach."

I don't let her say anything else before I grab her face, pulling it down to mine. The kiss is a slow glide that I feel all the way down to my dick. Her mouth opens to me, beckoning my tongue inside.

119

My tongue fucks her mouth, and I reach down to grip her hips, rubbing her up and down my cock to get it nice and wet.

I press her down harder on me. As the kiss intensifies, she makes these breathy little moans. If I move her just a tiny bit, I could be deep inside her. "Are you on the pill?"

"I have an IUD. Why?"

"Baby, I don't have any condoms. I'm safe, but I'll let you decide if you want to fuck without protection." I don't want her to feel like I'm pressuring her into anything. I'd be totally fine with her just grinding against me until we both came.

Shayla is quiet, but she reaches between us, lifts her hips, and then I feel her impale herself on my dick. "Ohhhh...*fuuuuuuck*," I moan. Right now I'm in heaven; she's hot, tight, and oh-so wet. "Fuck me, baby," I whisper.

Ever so slowly, she begins to rock back and forth, up and down. I reach around and grab her ass cheeks, holding her in place while I sit up. I place her feet next to my hips on both sides. A groan rips from my throat as I feel myself sink deeper inside her.

Shayla grabs my face and kisses my mouth. Her tongue slips inside, dancing with mine. She fucks me slowly, her arousal wetting my groin.

"You feel so good, baby," I whisper in between kisses.

"Yesssss," she moans, and then begins to increase her speed. I lift her enough to wrap my lips around her nipple, sucking it into my mouth. Her pussy clenches around my dick with each pull. I give the other breast the same treatment.

I remove one hand from her ass and reach between us, rubbing her clit. I know she's close to coming when her movements become erratic. "Give me your mouth when you come, baby." On her downward thrust, I thrust up and pinch her clit. She smashes her lips against mine as she comes hard, moaning into my mouth.

Two more thrusts and I groan as I empty inside her—the only time in my life that I've done that with someone. She wraps her arms around my shoulders and rests her head on my shoulder. "That was amazing," Shayla says against my neck.

"You got that right. That was off the charts ah-fucking-mazing." Once our breathing returns to normal, I pull her off my dick, grab my shirt from today, and use that to wipe us both off. I throw my boxer briefs back on while Shayla throws on her sweater and underwear.

"Happy Thanksgiving, Erik." She kisses the underside of my chin and snuggles in close. Just like before, she falls asleep almost immediately.

*****

I wake up and find that I'm alone. Staring up at the ceiling, last night flashes back through my mind. I've never, *ever* thought about taking someone without protection, but with her, there was no thinking about it. It felt good, it felt right. I climb out of bed and quickly shower before heading up upstairs. At the kitchen table I find my mom, Tad, Gretchen, Grant, and Shayla. "Good morning, everyone."

"Honey, your plate is in the oven, I didn't want your food to get cold. There's also fresh coffee." My mom, always the caretaker.

I grab my plate and take it to the table. I sit next to Shayla and grab her by the back of the neck, bringing her toward me for a quick kiss. My family is staring at us, I know this, but I don't really care. When I pull back, Shayla gives me a soft smile and then goes back to eating.

After breakfast I take Shayla and Grant home. She's quiet on the ride home, but she takes my hand when I hold it out to her. At noon we pull up in front of her place, and immediately I sense something is off. I pull into an open spot up the street. Shayla reaches for the handle, but I stop her.

"What's wrong?" She's looking around like she's expecting someone or something to show up.

I lean in close. "Your door to your apartment is open. Let me go check it out. As soon as I step out, I want you to lock the door behind me. Just promise me you'll sit tight."

"Yes, of course. Be careful," she tells me. I kiss her quickly and look in the back seat to see that Grant is oblivious to what's going on while he watches something on his device. Thank God for headphones.

The minute I shut the door behind me, I hear the locks engage. I bend down to "check my shoelaces"—in other words, I unsnap my ankle holster. I make my way toward her apartment, and my eyes never stop checking everything out. I move around to the back, checking the windows to her place. Luckily they all seem to be intact. Once I reach the door, I find Lucifer sitting right inside the door.

Thank God the cat didn't run off—I know how much Grant loves the furball. Pushing the door open slowly, I peer inside before I enter the apartment. Room by room, I move through her apartment and don't see anything out of place. Of course I haven't been here enough to know for sure.

After checking every nook and cranny, I head outside. When I inspect the lock it doesn't look like it's been tampered with, but there are kits out there now that make it hard to tell. I shut the door behind me, head to my Explorer, and let Shayla know it's safe to come in.

Until I know for sure what happened, I don't want her staying here. For her and Grant's safety, I'll have cameras installed as an added safeguard, but I don't want her returning until that's done. When they follow me inside, Grant runs past us and heads into the bathroom.

I pull Shayla into the kitchen. "Until I can get some cameras installed, I want you guys to stay with me." She opens her mouth to argue, but I hold my hand up. "I know it's not ideal, but I can't in good conscience let you stay here until I make sure it's absolutely safe."

The safety of the women in my life will always be my priority. I'll never forget watching Delilah give birth on the ground and how much she struggled at first. I'll be damned if that happens to anyone else.

"You both can stay in Gretchen's room if it's an

issue for you." I lean in close. "You know what happened to Delilah. I'm not going to risk your safety or Grant's. I'll even let you bring Lucifer."

She worries her bottom lip. "I'm a little freaked out right now."

I pull her into my arms. "Don't get freaked. It's probably nothing, but I just want to make sure of that, okay? We'll bring Grant to Luna every morning and then I'll take you to work."

"But what if you're busy with a case? I don't want you to make the extra trips just for me."

"There's a whole group of men who would be happy to come get you. You can go back to taking the L when I'm a hundred percent sure that your door being open was just a fluke. I know this is a lot, but please do this for me."

She reluctantly agrees, and while she gets a bag ready for her and Grant, I take care of Lucifer. He immediately starts crying when I stick him in the cat carrier. Shayla and Grant come walking out a few minutes later with their bags over their shoulders. Grant drops his bag by the door and gets down in front of the cage.

"Luci, it's okay. We're going on a little twip." The kid is freaking adorable.

"Are you guys ready?" I pick up Lucifer's carrier and wait for Grant and Shayla to step out. I shut the door, pushing on it to make sure it's not going to open. We head down to my Explorer, and while we walk I shoot a quick text to Egan.

Erik: Hey man, when you're free I need security cameras put in at Shayla's. When I

brought them home her door was open. Luckily I didn't find anything. She and her son are staying with me until I know it's safe.

I stick my phone back in my coat pocket and load Lucifer into the back so his door is facing Grant. Shayla buckles him in, and then hops in the front. She's quiet on the drive to my place, and even Grant seems to be lost in thought. I glance at him in the rearview mirror and smile. He looks just like his mom.

For a little boy, his expression is so serious. I'm hoping this time at my place he'll get to know me and not be so quiet or skittish around me. I pull into a spot down from my apartment, and we grab Lucifer and the bags, heading into my building. In Gretchen's room, I set Lucifer's carrier on the bed and let him out.

***

I walk next to Shayla as she pushes the cart up and down the aisles at Whole Foods. One thing about being a bachelor is I usually eat out, but now with them staying with me, I need *everything*. Grant walks on the other side of her. Our cart is full with lots of healthy food, and the deal was I buy and she cooks.

She didn't completely agree with me, but I want to take care of them. I'm stubborn, and wouldn't have given up. When we get in line at the checkout, I can feel eyes on me. I turn and find a busty redhead giving me "fuck me" eyes. Normally, I'd find someplace to fuck her and then be on my way.

But now...now I feel nothing. I look down at Shayla to see her glaring daggers at the redhead. Why does it get me hot that she's pissed off and looks like she wants to pounce on the other woman?

I throw my arm around her shoulders and hug her into my side. Leaning down, I whisper in her ear, "You're the only one I see, baby."

"I suppose this is something that happens everywhere you go?"

"I can't help it I'm sexy—yeah, baby." I give her my best Austin Powers impression.

She rolls her eyes, but then laughs softly as she starts putting the groceries on the belt. I look down at Grant, and he's smiling as he looks at both his mom and me. "Your mom thinks I'm silly. What do you think—am I silly?"

He looks at me closely, and then nods. I give myself a mental high-five.

One we pay for the groceries, we take them home and put them away. During dinner, which consisted of turkey hot dogs cut up in macaroni and cheese, I make sure she knows that whatever their routine is, it's fine with me. "Seriously, whatever you need to do, just do it. I don't want Grant's schedule getting screwed up."

"Thank you," she says quietly. My eyes go to Grant, who shovels his food in like he's never had anything better. To be honest it is pretty good, and in order to keep eating like this I'm going to have to hit the gym. Of course I could make my own meals, but that would be rude.

After we eat, I tell her that I'll clean up so she

can get Grant cleaned up for bed. My phone dings while I'm loading the dishwasher, and I see it's a text from Egan.

Egan: You moved them in, huh? You work fast, not as fast as Reece though.

I shake my head as I see the dots dance again.

Egan: On a serious note I've got time to stop by there Monday morning. Just drop me off a set of her keys. We'll stay out of her room, but put one in Grant's. I'll make sure they're set up. We'll monitor through Rogue too.

Erik: Thanks brother. Send the bill to me for the equipment. Don't let Carrie know, she'll tell Shayla.

Egan: You got it. You've got it bad for her…I like it.

I don't send a response because that dickhead is just fishing for answers. I knew he'd be all over helping Shayla.

I hear Shayla and Grant's laughter from the bathroom, and it makes me realize what I've been missing in my life.

CHAPTER TWELVE

Shayla

"I love you, Grunt." I bend down and kiss my baby boy's forehead. "Mommy will be in later."

His arms wrap around my shoulders, holding me tightly to him. "I love you too." Grant finally lets me up, and I smile down at him.

Lucifer moves into the spot I vacate when I stand up. I blow Grant a kiss, and he catches it then hugs it to his chest. It makes me smile, and I turn to walk out of the room. Erik stands in the doorway—his eyes are soft as they watch me. When I reach him, he looks over my shoulder. "Goodnight, Grant." My little boy just stares at Erik, and then rolls over.

In the hall, I look up at him after I shut the door. "I'm sorry," I whisper.

He cups my cheeks in both of his large palms. "Don't be sorry. He'll warm up to me when he's ready." Erik leans down, kissing my lips softly.

The kiss goes on for a while until he finally pulls back. "I'm going to head to the gym—it's just down on the corner. I want you to lock the deadbolt behind me. I'll have my keys to get back in." He picks up his gym bag off the floor, grabs my hand, and walks me into the living room. "I'll be back in an hour or so."

"Okay. Have fun." Erik kisses my lips one more time before he leaves. I do as he requested and lock the door.

After checking on Grant, I curl up on the couch with my Kindle. I'm reading the latest Kristen Ashley book, and since it's so easy to get lost in her stories I lose all track of time. The next thing I know, Erik's stepping into the apartment. I close my cover and sit up. "How was your workout?"

He sits down next to me and pulls me onto his lap. "It was good, but I've got a way I'd rather get a good workout in." Erik kisses my neck, making me squeal. It causes goosebumps to pop up all over my body.

I slap at his chest. "You're bad."

"I have to shower. Wanna come scrub my back?" Erik stands up with me in his arms and carries me down the hall into his bedroom.

"What about Grant?" We haven't done anything since we've been here. I worry about him hearing us.

"Was he asleep?" I nod. "Then baby, he's not going to wake up. Plus if he does, I'll hear him."

I kiss him and let him carry me into the bathroom, where we proceed to get each other *very* dirty, and then *very* clean.

***

"How long are you going to be staying with him?" I'm at Luna's dropping Grant off. Erik is sitting in his SUV waiting for me.

"Egan is installing cameras in the apartment, and they're going to change my lock. This is all just a precaution. We should be home by this weekend," I say, shrugging. I know it's only been a few days, but I've loved spending time with Erik. He has so many layers I've loved uncovering. He's funny, sweet, good with my kid, and patient with said kid.

Luna misses nothing. "Why does it look like someone took your favorite toy?" She smiles at me. "You really like him."

I bite my lip. "Yes, and it scares the shit out of me."

"Oh, honey…" She wraps her arms around me. "It's understandable, so just take your time. Get to know each other; let Grant get used to him. This is a good thing, I can feel it."

After hugging her, Grant, and the girls goodbye, I run out to the Explorer; once I hop in and shut the door, I turn to Erik. "Sorry, I was talking to her about the security cameras being installed and stuff."

"That's okay. I had a couple of phone calls to make." We head toward downtown and our office. I hop out as soon as he parks in the garage.

We head upstairs, and I stop to talk to Carrie while Erik disappears into the back. "How's it going staying with Erik?"

"It's an adjustment, but it's been good. Did Egan tell you what happened?" I'm not sure if everyone knows or not.

Carrie nods. "Egan mentioned that he was going to install cameras. Do you think someone broke into your place?"

Do I? No, I know Ryan's no longer in jail, but he hasn't made any attempt to contact me. He's moved on, thank god. Oh fuck, but then in thinking it's not him, I'm just like those heroines in the romance novels I read, and he'll end up being the bad guy. But...none of our stuff was messed with, Lucifer wasn't gone, and no one was there when we got home.

I shake my head. "No, I think when we were leaving I just didn't shut it tightly. Lucifer didn't leave the apartment, so I think it had happened shortly before we got home."

"Well, that's good. The cameras will at least give you peace of mind. I think they're all still on edge after what happened to Delilah."

We talk about having lunch together and then I head to my office—well, Delilah's office, when she comes back. After dumping my stuff, I head into the break room for a cup of coffee. Surprisingly, I find the room empty. After pouring a cup, I head down the hall. When I get close to Erik's office, I hear him talking. I know I shouldn't stop and listen, but I do.

"Hey darlin', I got your message that you're back in town. I'm sorry I can't hook up." There's a pause. "Yeah, I'm seeing someone." He chuckles, and it's a rich sound. "Of course she's gorgeous. She's got a beautiful heart, and the most adorable son."

His door is cracked open a little, but he can't see

me as I race by and head to my office so I can get to work.

When the day is over, I collect my stuff, put my coat on, and go searching for Erik. I see that he's nowhere to be found. I stop at Jack's open office door. "Hi, Jack. Have you seen Erik?"

The older man smiles up at me. "Hey, I was just getting ready to come find you. Erik is out working on something with Reece. I'm going to give you a ride to your babysitter's place, and Erik will pick you up there."

"Okay, thanks Jack."

I wait out in the reception area for him to join me a few minutes later. We ride the elevators in silence, and that's okay. This man, though he's nice, intimidates the hell out of me. He leads me to a—surprise, surprise—black Escalade. What is it with men and their black SUVs?

As I buckle my belt, I don't miss the base for a baby carrier strapped to the back seat. I smile because from what Delilah's told me, he's absolutely smitten with his granddaughter, and sometimes he'll come take her just for a little bit so Delilah can nap.

When we stop at a traffic light, Jack fiddles with his phone and then holds it up. "Charlie smiled yesterday." I take his phone and smile at the picture. Oh sure, it *looks* like she's smiling, but at only a month old, it's more than likely gas.

"She's a doll. I'm glad Delilah seems to be doing better." I hand him his phone back.

"You and me both. I'm just glad she has someone like Reece looking out for her. You're a parent—you know what it's like to do whatever's necessary to look out for our kids." His words make my stomach dip. Why? Because I took Ryan's abuse for too long before I finally left.

That night comes back to me, and the horrified look on Grant's face when he walked in and saw Ryan beating me. Tears slid down his face, but he made no noise while he stood there. The underlying guilt I always feel comes roaring back, strong as ever.

I thank Jack for the ride and hop out. On quick feet I make my way up to Luna and Rocco's apartment. When Luna opens the door, she holds her finger to her lips and leads me into their kitchen. What I see makes my heart trip up in my chest. Erik is here already and at the table with Grant, who's sitting right next to him on one side with Lennon on the other. Their heads are all bent and they're coloring together.

He must feel my eyes on him because he looks up and gives me that smile that makes my belly dip. In all honesty he looks ridiculous, but only because he's so large and the kids are so little. Erik leans toward Grant and whispers something. My boy looks up, and when he sees me he smiles. Of course as always the guilt curdles in my belly.

Grant climbs down from his chair and comes running toward me. "Hi, Mommy."

"Hi, my baby boy. Did you have a good day?"

He wraps his arms around my thighs and then tips his head back to look up at me. "I did. Erik and me are coloring you a picture."

"It's Erik and I, baby." He nods and then runs

133

back over to the table.

Starr runs over to me, and I pick her up. "Hi, sweetheart."

I greet Luna's girls while Erik and Grant finish coloring. Once they're done, they present both pictures to me. "I'll look at these in the car."

We take our leave, and on the way home I look at the pictures on my lap and smile. Erik's picture is just a bunch of flowers. As he drives toward his place, he leans toward me. "Now you can say I've given you flowers."

"Thank you for the flowers," I tell him before pulling out Grant's picture. Immediately my eyes burn. It's a picture of a woman and little boy holding hands. Of course they're stick figures and they're holding hands. On the other side of the little boy is a cat. I turn to look at Grant. "Thanks for the picture, baby."

Back at Erik's, I get set up in the kitchen to make dinner. I take a moment while I'm alone to push those feelings of guilt away. They don't help me—I can't change the past as much as I might want to, and I just need to move forward. It's *so* fucking hard, though.

I make my special baked chicken strips, sweet potato fries, and a huge salad for dinner. We sit around the kitchen table and I watch both my boy and Erik clean their plates and then some. My ex was a big man, though not as big as Erik, and the men are big in my family too, so Grant has no choice but to be huge.

"Grant, I was talking to Gretchen earlier, and she wants to see you so she's coming to spend the night with us this coming weekend. If I set up an air mattress in your bedroom, do you think she could sleep in there with you?"

I watch my son look at Erik with no expression and my stomach starts to knot, but then it's like a miracle happens. Grant's lips tip up into a smile, albeit a small one, and he nods his head. "Yep." That's all he says to him, but I'll take it because it means he's warming up to him.

"Good. She'll be happy to hear that." My little Grunt goes back to eating and only shrugging when Erik talks to him.

When I look at Erik, he gives me a wink. I lick my lips nervously. My heart pounds in my chest and I feel a flush creeping up my cheeks. I know I'm in big trouble because I want to crawl on his lap and kiss the shit out of him. Instead of that, I look down at my plate until I have myself back under control.

"Egan got the cameras installed, but we want to watch things for at least another week before you guys are good to stay there again." That makes my stomach clench, but I push it back while swallowing the knot in my throat.

I look up at him and nod. "We can go stay at a hotel if it's easier on you. I know we're cramping your style."

"You're *not* cramping my style. You'll stay with me until it's fine for you to go back." I can hear the conviction in his voice. Plus he's never been anything other than honest with me.

"Thank you, Erik."

***

Erik bites my neck, and I moan.

It wasn't long after Grant went to bed that we began making out in the kitchen. I couldn't help myself—he'd gone to the gym earlier, and when he'd come home he'd gone to shower. I'd decided to make him a protein shake, and when he'd come out to get it, he'd only been wearing a towel. The man is gorgeous fully clothed, but in just a towel around his hips…no words could describe it.

His muscles were bulging, and behind the towel I could see the big bulge of his dick. Next thing I knew I was in his arms with my legs wrapped around his waist.

Now my back is against the headboard and my legs are again wrapped around him as he pounds into me. I feel those familiar tingles begin as my orgasm comes racing toward the surface.

"*Fuuuucck*…you're squeezing me so fucking tight," he whispers against my ear.

I whimper as he nips my earlobe. He braces one hand on the wall and reaches between us with the other, strumming my clit until I have to bite my lip to stop from crying out as I come, and hard. While I continue to come Erik flips us, pushes my legs back and pounds into me until he buries himself to the hilt.

He pulls his softening cock from me and kisses my lips softly. "I'll be right back." He disappears into his bathroom while I slip my panties and nightgown on. A minute later, the toilet flushes and the sink turns on and off. Erik climbs back into bed with pajama pants on and pulls me to him. "It keeps getting better and better with you," he whispers softly against my forehead.

I burrow under his chin. "There are things about me that I haven't told you yet, but…I'm not ready."

"I know baby, and I know you'll tell me when you're ready." We lie chest to chest, and he strokes my cheek as his bedroom is bathed in moonlight. "This weekend I thought we could go get a Christmas tree. The kids can decorate it." My heart squeezes. I like the sound of that—"the kids"—so much. Maybe *too* much.

"That sounds like a lot of fun. We could grab the lights and decorations I have at my place. It's not a lot, but it's a good start."

We lie there for a long time, kissing, talking, or just cuddling. "What's one of your fondest memories of your dad?" I ask him.

For a second I think I may have said the wrong thing because his body stiffens, but then he relaxes. "I was eight, and it was about a year before he died. He and my Uncle Chet had taken me and my cousins to our first Cubs game. I remember we sat in the bleachers, and we gorged ourselves on hot dogs, popcorn, and cotton candy. We were having the best time, and the ultimate happened." He laughs softly.

"Mark Grace hit a homer, and we could see it coming right toward us. I held up my glove, and he lifted me in the air. The ball hit my hand so hard, but when my dad lowered me to the ground and I turned my hand over and saw that baseball in my glove, we jumped up and down. We were so excited, my dad took me down and after the game Mark signed my ball." Erik gets quiet for a minute.

"At his funeral I stuck the ball in his casket, and he was buried with it."

I say nothing but wrap my arms around him, hugging him close. "Thank you for sharing that with me."

He hugs me back. "I miss him so fucking much. I've forgotten so much about him." Erik clutches me to him in a firm grip.

To see this big man vulnerable is bringing me to my knees. I'm not sure how long we lie here before Erik's breathing evens out, and I know he's asleep. I listen to his deep breathing, and it doesn't take long before it lulls me to sleep.

Opening my eyes, I realize I'm in Erik's bed, facing the wrong direction, and I'm alone. I head into his bathroom, and once I'm finished I head out into the living room, but it's empty.

"Can I stir it?" I hear Grant's voice.

"Yeah bud, nice and slow, okay?"

I peer around the corner; Erik is in front of the stove flipping a pancake while Grant stirs something in a big red bowl. "I'm doing it." My son smiles at Erik, and when he sees me he flings his arms up, getting batter everywhere. "Look Mommy, I'm making bweakfast."

I come up behind my boy, wrapping my arms around him. "I see that. You're doing a great job." I kiss the top of his head and then wrap my arms around Erik. "Good morning."

Erik leans down, kissing my lips gently before standing back up. "Morning." He's quiet, not his usual flirtatious self. I never should've mentioned his dad. Maybe he's upset with me for bringing it up.

My heart starts to race, and an unwelcome feeling slithers down my spine. When Ryan used to get mad, and before he started using his fists, he would play the mental game with me—ignoring me or berating me.

I take a deep breath and push those feelings aside. Erik is *not* Ryan, and he's treated me with nothing but kindness…and shameless flirting

After he finishes making the pancakes, we all sit together and begin to eat. Grant's quiet, but that's only because he's shoveling food into his mouth. Erik finishes up first, and after he puts his plate in the sink, he disappears down the hall.

"Baby, I'll be right back. I'm going to talk to Erik." He nods and goes back to shoveling his food in.

Lucifer watches me from the couch as I follow after Erik. His door is open and I hear a noise coming from his closet. A moment later, he comes out with a binder in his hands. "Come here, baby." Erik sits on the end of the bed and pats the spot next to him.

"I'm sorry I brought up your dad. I didn't mean—"

He holds up his hand. "No, I'm glad you did. I forgot that my mom made this for me and sent it the first time I was deployed." Erik flips it open—it's a scrapbook of him and his mom and Dad.

Grant joins us a minute later with a sticky mouth and sits on my lap while Erik shows us the pictures and tells us the story behind them. He remembers so much about his dad, more than he realized. By the time he's done, my head is resting on his shoulder. "You should keep it on your bookcase."

He seems to perk up a little after the trip down memory lane, and after his shower. While he gets dressed, I shower in the other room. It's not a hair-washing day, so I'm ready in twenty minutes. The temperature is even more frigid today. Erik and Grant wear matching beanies on their heads, but it was the only way I could get Grant to wear a hat.

In such a short time my son is really warming up to Erik, which is great, because every day I'm falling harder and harder for this man.

After we drop Grant off we stop in my apartment, and he shows me where all the cameras are; I'm glad no one will see me in my room. He explains that after Grant and I go to sleep, the cameras will go into sleep mode, only turning back on if they sense movement. Erik also tells me that the cameras are high enough that the cat won't trigger them.

While we're here, I grab some more clothes and the Christmas decorations.

Once we get to the office, he kisses me before he disappears toward the conference room. When I get into my office, I get to work.

CHAPTER THIRTEEN

Erik

I grab Shayla's hand and pull her in between two Douglas fir trees, kissing the shit out of her. The rest of this past week I hardly got to see her due to a case that I was working on. Luckily between Reece, Jack, and Egan, they've helped me get my girl and her boy home to my place. She was usually asleep by the time I got home, but she usually left me a note and instructions for how to warm up my plate of food she had waiting for me.

She also had started sleeping in my bed, even without me. All I would have to do is strip off my clothes and then crawl into bed, pulling her into my arms. This girl has me wanting things I've always figured I'd never have, because what if something happened to me and I left my wife to raise our children alone? I just couldn't do that to someone I loved.

I pull back and smile down at her. "I *really* needed that."

"Me too," she says with a sigh.

141

I grab her hand and pull her out from between the trees. We spot the kids up ahead, grab them, and head over to the concession stand for hot chocolates for the kids and Shayla. I get myself a hot cider.

It's been the perfect fucking day. Tad and my mom dropped Gretchen off at eight this morning. Grant had been up since six, anxiously waiting for her arrival. When she arrived, Grant went downstairs with me to get her. It's amazing the bond they share already.

We took the kids out for breakfast before we came to the tree farm, which brings us to now. There's a Santa here, and somehow my sister convinces me that we need to get our picture taken with him. After we drink our beverages, we head over to the jolly man in the red suit. Gretchen takes Grant up to sit on Santa's lap so he can tell him what he wants for Christmas.

When he's finished, I drag Shayla with me and sit next to Santa on the red bench. I pull her to sit on my lap, and we all smile at the camera. While the girls and Grant wait for the picture to print out, I go pay for the tree and they put it through the little machine that ties it up.

They meet me at the Explorer, and Shayla holds the photo out to me. I take it from her and turn it over for a look. "*Wow*" is all I can say. We look perfect, and it makes me fall that much harder for her, and that much more for that little boy. I look up at her and smile. "We need to frame this."

She nods. "That's why I got this." Shayla holds up a picture frame that's red and covered in hand-painted snowflakes.

Her lips tip up at the corners, and I bend down to kiss those lips.

When we get back to the apartment we get the tree set up and I wrap it in the lights before Shayla and the kids do the decorating. Once the girls are finished, we decide to walk down the street to a little pizzeria.

When we sit down, they come out to take our drink orders and then our order for food. I glance out the window and spot a man standing across the street just staring at us. His face isn't recognizable to me, but that doesn't mean anything. I move to stand up and go outside, but when I turn back, he's gone. "I'll be right back," I tell Shayla as I slip my coat on.

"Is everything okay?" she asks.

"Yeah babe, I just need to check something real quick." I step outside and look up and down the street but don't see him.

It was probably some jackass checking my woman out. I head inside and am just slipping my coat off when they deliver some fresh, hot garlic bread for us. When our pie comes, my mouth immediately waters.

We were definitely all hungry because we're quiet while we eat. When we finally finish, they box up our leftovers and we head back to my apartment.

***

Shayla and Grant stayed back at my place while I took Gretchen home. Shayla wanted my sister and I to have some quality time together. "If you don't marry Shayla, I'm gonna kick your butt."

I turn my head to look at my sister and can't help but laugh. She looks serious as hell right now. "It's a little too soon to think about marriage, but I'm falling in love with her." Gretchen squeals and does that girly clap while hopping up and down in her seat.

We pull into the driveway of my parents' home, and Gretchen opens the door. I follow her inside. "Mom! Tad! We're here." I holler, and hear my mom yell they're in the kitchen. They're sitting at the breakfast bar eating lunch. I hug my mom and slap Tad on the shoulder. "How was your sermon today?" Tad's always respected the fact that I'm not the church-going type.

"It was good. The congregation is definitely getting in the Christmas spirit. If they're free, are you bringing Shayla and Grant for Christmas?"

"I haven't asked her, but I was planning on it." Tad always does the sermon on Christmas Eve, and the kids sing for the congregation. It's one of the few times Tad gets me in there. They know I sometimes have a hard time seeing Cesar, but I do it because it's important to my mom.

"Oh honey, that would be wonderful. It's been so long since I've had a little one around for Christmas morning. Gretch, we could make your favorite breakfast casserole. I bet he'd love it. Oh, and Christmas Eve morning we could make the cookies we'll put out for Santa." I knew she'd be preparing to go overboard, but Grant deserves that and so much more.

I only stay for a little while longer before I head

toward home…*home*. Now that I have them in my place, I have to figure out a way to never let them go.

***

I follow the silver BMW across town. I've been tailing this guy for a week, and he's finally leading me to something. This week the douchebag I've been tailing has led me to his mistress's place, the gym, and a travel agent. Now I've hit pay dirt. I was hired by this guy's employer—they suspect he's stealing designs and then selling them to their main competitor.

He pulls into the parking lot of a Starbucks in Oak Brook. I can see now why they chose this location—it's busy as fuck. I let the douche go inside before I hop out of my Explorer and make my way inside. Inside, he's two people in front of me in line. To a layman, he appears to be just your average guy at Starbucks for a meeting.

What *I* see, though, is a man whose pulse is pounding in his neck, who's clutching his messenger bag so tight his knuckles are white. I don't miss the way his eyes flit around the space. The fucker is nervous, and he should be, because as soon as I catch him handing off the flash drive, his boss is going to call him in and let him know the plans aren't the real ones.

The douche signed an agreement when he got hired that clearly stated that if he was caught sharing information, then it was immediate termination and legal action. The guy might be getting paid for the plans, but that'll all just be sucked into legal fees...dumbass.

After I get my coffee, I sit down across from him. He keeps looking out the window. Is he *trying* to give himself away? While I wait, I send Shayla a quick text.

> **Erik: Hey babe, do you want me to pick up a pizza for dinner?**

The dots start bouncing, and I wait eagerly for her to respond.

> **Shayla: I'm actually making a meatloaf, homemade mashed potatoes and peas.**

> **Erik: You don't have to cook every day, you know that right? You work full-time too, and do everything for Grant.**

The dots start bouncing again.

> **Shayla: I know I don't but it was always so hard cooking for just the two of us. I like doing it.**

> **Erik: Okay well I'm not complaining because you're an amazing cook.**

> **Shayla: Thanks, oh, I invited Dalton to stay for dinner.**

When one of the other guys has to pick her up

and take her and Grant back to my place, she usually invites them to stay for dinner. So far she's fed Marcus, Jack, and Dalton.

The douche's body tenses, so I focus back on what I'm doing. I open my camera app and wait. The guy who comes inside is short but built, reminding me of a bulldog. He sits down next to the douche, and they begin whispering to each other. I take picture after picture until I get the money shot: the douche handing over the flash drive to the bulldog.

I finish my coffee and escape out to my Explorer. On my way home, I call my contact to let him know that I'll be sending him the information when I get home. I reach my street and find a place to park. I grab my bag and hop out. On the sidewalk, I'm looking down at my phone, not watching where I'm going when I bump into someone.

I look up. "Sorry, man."

He just nods and starts walking away. Why does he look familiar? I turn and look for him, but he's disappeared. I shake off the on-edge feeling that guy gives me. I enter my building, riding the elevator to my floor. As soon as I step off the elevator, the scent of meatloaf hits me, and my mouth begins to water.

When I step inside, I freeze. Shayla's standing in the middle of the living room. I shut the door behind me. "What's going on? Is Grant okay? I thought Dalton was coming."

"Yes, sorry he's fine, and I asked Dalton to reschedule. Right after I texted you Luna called and asked if Grant could sleep over. They were going to come get him and then go get pizza. I thought maybe we could…we could talk about stuff."

She seems very scared to tell me whatever it is. I almost don't want to know what it is if it's already upsetting her, but I know if we're going to have a future, then we need to be able to talk about this kind of stuff—our dirty laundry, so to speak. I've already talked to her about my dad.

I walk to her and pull her into my arms. "I told you that you could tell me when you're ready."

"I know, and I'm ready now, but let's eat first."

We sit at the kitchen table and are both silent while we eat. I moan around the first bite. "This shit is amazing."

She smiles at me, and then places her fork down, her smile falling. "The first time Ryan hit me, he knocked my front tooth out. I left him, and my brother beat his ass. He came back a week later, crying and saying that he'd never done that before. I was stupid and took him back."

I push my plate away and reach across the table, grabbing for her hand, but she jerks it away from me and places both hands in her lap. "It took six months before he hit me again, and it was because I found out he'd slept with someone else the week we were apart, and I got upset.

"It was right after that when I found out I was pregnant. He was okay when I was pregnant, and only slapped me a few times, and then toward the end, he controlled what and how much I ate." My stomach knots as she goes on to tell me about how he'd get jealous that she was spending more time

148

with Grant—their *baby*—and that he'd had tons of flings.

"By the time Grant was born, my parents and brother quit speaking to me. They said they weren't going to watch me slowly die. Notice they didn't even offer to protect me from him if I wanted to leave. The final straw was a little over two years ago. One of his 'girlfriends' approached me in front of Grant, talking about how my husband liked to fuck her hard and dirty." Her eyes glisten, and she takes a deep breath.

"When he got home, I'd put Grant to bed and confronted him. He punched me in the face, knocking me to the bed. He'd gone crazy, hitting and biting all over my body. Grant had walked in and saw me covered in blood and bruises. He was scared to talk after that day for a while, and now he's leery of men until he gets to know them."

I move my chair around the table until I'm right next to her. I cradle her hands in between mine and bring them to my chest. "Did you ever try to contact your family after you left him?"

She nods. "As soon as I left, I went to the police and pressed charges against Ryan, and then I took Grant with me to my parents' house. My dad took one look at me and Grant and sh-shut the door in my face." Her chin wobbles. A lone tear leaves a silvery trail as it slides down her face, but she's silent.

"I s-stayed with that monster when I should've run far, far away from him, but I didn't because I was weak. Do you think I'm a bad person for staying?" I hate how small her voice sounds right now.

"Fuck no, baby. Men like him are really good at making women feel like their only option is to stay. The point is, you left. You protected yourself and your son from a monster." I can tell the walls I was working to knock down are starting to reform...*fucking shit.*

Shayla wipes angrily at the tears running down her cheeks. "Do you know how long he had to serve?" I shake my head. "*Six months,* that's it. And he only got that because the lawyers I worked for were amazing and helped me get him locked up. They could've gotten longer, but I never reported the other incidents, so it was his first offense."

"When's the last time you saw him?"

"Two years ago, when I served him with divorce papers, and I'm not sure why he agreed so easy or why he didn't try to fight me to see Grant once he was out. He hasn't bothered us since."

She lays her head on my shoulder, and I hug her tightly to my chest. Silence surrounds us, and I can't believe anyone could hurt her.

"Sorry for bringing this up now, and right before Christmas. Nothing says holiday spirit like bringing skeletons out of the closet. I-I just care about you a lot, and I don't know...I just thought you should have all the information about me. Now you know why Grant's the way he is."

"I've been waiting for you to open up, and I didn't care when you did it. I just wanted you to trust me enough that you felt comfortable." That seems to be the right answer, because I feel the moment she relaxes against me.

Even though I'm fucking furious at the thought of her piece of shit ex-husband hurting her and Grant this much, my heart feels so fucking full knowing she trusts me with the whole truth. I realize it's time for me to do the same—trust her with my *own* demons.

I swallow against the lump in my throat. "I know you asked me in the beginning about whether I'd ever been deployed, and you respected that I didn't want to talk about it...I *still* hate talking about it, but it's never easy. You're away from home, the people you love...Conditions can sometimes be rough, but you quickly realize that you're so lucky compared to all the people you see out there starving, dying, and that makes you want to fight even harder for the people who can't. Plus, those Marines you spend every day with...they become family. I was lucky and never lost anyone from my unit, but I know others who lost *everyone*. The things you see, and the things you do...they stick with you long after the fighting is over. But Tad got me to speak to someone right away and it helped." I take a deep breath. "Anyway, I just wanted to share that."

Shayla says nothing—she just hugs me a little bit tighter.

CHAPTER FOURTEEN

Shayla

Today is Christmas Eve, and we're on our way up to Erik's parents' home. They were so sweet to invite Grant and me to spend the holiday with them. How amazing that since we moved to Chicago we've had so many people supporting us, helping us, and including us in family stuff. We may not have a family that's blood, but we do have a family of the heart.

It's only been a few days since I told Erik about my ex, and he's shown me nothing but support and care, proving that I made the right decision in opening my heart to this man. Yes, he may be a cocky flirt, but he's also kind, supportive, and loyal. He's the whole package, and he wants me, which I still can't believe, but he's proved over and over that he does.

I look behind me and smile at my boy. In his hand is a gift he wrapped himself that he picked out for Gretchen. It's a little snow globe with Tinkerbell in it. The best part is that Grant and Erik went to get it without me. That was a huge step, and Erik said that Grant even talked to him a little bit without Erik coaxing him.

This morning we wrapped the gift—or, Grant did. I just cut the paper and handed him the pieces of tape. In the back end of the Explorer are the rest of the gifts. Erik said he usually gave out gift cards, but I made him shop for real gifts with me. I think he had the most fun shopping for Grant, even though I told him he didn't need to get him anything. My son will be having Nerf gun wars for a long time.

For his Santa gifts I got Grant some books, a new tablet, and the new *Cars* movie. Plus with what Erik picked out, Grant is making out like a bandit. The previous two Christmases were hard, and money was tight, but Grant didn't seem to mind. Erik has asked me a few times what I wanted, but I dodged the question. It's been years since anyone's bought me a gift.

Luna asked me the first year we met, but I told her she could get something for Grant. I, of course, get stuff for her girls. Just like this year too. For his parents I wasn't sure what to get, so Erik helped me decide. We got his mom a Pandora bracelet, and Tad tickets to the season opener for the Cubs.

We pull into the driveway an hour later, and I grab Grant out of the back. Tad and Nicole come out to greet us. Tad helps Erik grab the bags while Nicole loops her arm through mine and leads me into the house. "Thank you for inviting Grant and me to spend the holiday with your family."

"Oh sweetheart, we're happy to have you here."

She hugs my arm as we step inside the house. Soft Christmas music plays in the background. Their tree is huge and brightly decorated. Grant walks in behind us, clutching the gift in his hands.

When Erik comes in with Tad, they place all the gifts under the tree. The Santa gifts will be hidden in Erik's room until Grant's asleep.

While we wait for the rest of their family to get here, we eat some hors d'oeuvres. Tonight after dinner, we're going to Tad's church for a Christmas Eve service, and I'm nervous. I've never really been the church-going type. Ryan and I got married by an ordained minister in a park by our home. He was choosing not to be traditional, but maybe it was also because he was evil and worried God would strike him dead if he walked into a church.

Maybe we should've done that and then I wouldn't have had to worry anymore since he'd be a grease spot.

***

I straighten Grant's sweater after I take his coat off in the vestibule of the church. It's such a beautiful place—it's small, but modern and homey. I hang up his coat before taking off mine and hanging it up too. He holds onto my hand tightly as people mill around. We get lots of curious looks, but with the size of the church, they probably all know each other.

Erik comes walking toward us and my mouth waters. He's in a dark gray suit with an ocean blue button-up shirt and no tie. I don't miss the appreciative glances some of these women give him, but he doesn't even seem to notice. Instead, he wraps his arm around my waist, kissing my lips.

The service is beautiful, and the songs are great. Gretchen and two other girls sing "Silent Night" a cappella, and it gives me chills. The girl looks like an angel and has a voice like one too. Once the service is over, I look down and see that Grant has fallen asleep. Without a second thought, Erik picks my boy up so he's sleeping on his shoulder.

We hang back, letting the other members of the congregation greet Tad. A man walks up to Tad's side, and I don't miss the way Erik stiffens. It dawns on me that it must be Cesar, the man who shot and killed Erik's dad.

I imagine it's hard to be around him, and even though the man paid for his crime, he's still here and Erik's dad isn't. I wrap my arm around his waist, giving him a reassuring squeeze. We make our way down the aisle when I freeze, my body going stiff. *No*, that's not possible, but in the back pew…I swear to God I'm looking at my ex-husband.

I squeeze my eyes shut, and when I open them, the man sitting there looks nothing like Ryan. Ugh…I know this is only because I told Erik all about Ryan earlier in the week. This occasionally happens and it'll fade by next week.

"You okay?" Erik leans down and asks against my ear.

I smile up at him. "Yeah, I think I'm just tired."

When we reach Tad, Nicole, and Cesar, all eyes are on us and the sleeping boy in Erik's arms. I hug his mom and then Tad. The other man holds out his hand and introduces himself to me. I take it, giving it a quick shake. He doesn't hold out his hand to Erik—Cesar just gives him a chin lift and Erik does the same. Gretchen joins us a few minutes later, lightening the mood, and her little girlfriends all stare at Erik like he's a dream come to life.

We say our goodbyes and take Gretchen back to his parents' home. Grant wakes up on the way. Once we get back, Grant and Gretchen set out the milk and cookies for Santa. After getting him ready for bed, I get him tucked in, and he's so tired he's asleep before I'm even to the door. When I get back downstairs, everyone else is back. I sit next to Erik on the couch and snuggle into him. I grab one of the cookies, making sure to leave crumbs on the plate. I open my mouth to take a bite, but it's ripped from my hand.

Erik winks at me before taking a huge bite. He holds what's left out to me. "Did you want this?" I snatch it back and shove the rest in my mouth, not even caring how unladylike it is. He just hugs me into his side.

Nicole brings out a bottle of champagne and pours us all a glass. "It's going to be so nice having a little one here for Christmas."

"Thank you again for having us. That was so kind of you to include us."

"Oh, absolutely, sweetheart—we're happy that Erik's finally found someone *special* to bring home." Erik mutters something under his breath, and his mom smiles at me.

"We should get the gifts out of the back," Tad

says to me before going out with Erik to get them all.

When they come back inside, I help place the gifts under the tree. While arranging them, I see several with my name on the tag from his mom, and my eyes begin to burn. These people are a dream, and I've never felt more like part of a family.

My son is not going to know what to do with himself in the morning. On that thought, I say goodnight to everyone and head downstairs to Erik's room. I throw on some red leggings with white snowflakes on them and an off-the-shoulder green long-sleeved t-shirt with a red camisole underneath.

I'm just braiding my hair when Erik comes down. He looks me up and down and smiles widely. "Love the jammies."

"Thank you." I watch him through the mirror in the bathroom as he strips out of his suit and down to his boxer briefs. As always, my mouth waters when I take in the hotness that is him. All ripped muscle, lightly tanned skin, and the most beautiful cock I've ever seen.

He throws on a pair of sweatpants that sit low on his narrow waist, highlighting that fucking V that makes grown women stupid. I quickly brush my teeth and wash my face. When I come into the bedroom, I rub my moisturizer on my face as Erik goes into the bathroom to take care of his business. I climb under the covers and snuggle into the bed. I'm so exhausted that I'm asleep before Erik even comes to bed.

***

I'm up the minute I hear the pounding of little feet. I hop out of bed and head into the bathroom to take care of business and brush my teeth. When I'm bent over spitting the foam into the sink, I feel Erik's strong arms wrap around me. "Merry Christmas, baby." He kisses my neck.

I turn in his arms, and he kisses me deeply and thoroughly. "Merry Christmas," I say breathlessly.

The door to the basement opens, and I hear Gretchen call down, "Come on, guys! Santa was here and Grant's ready to open presents whether we're there or not."

The door shuts, and I look up at Erik and laugh. "We better head up there before he just starts opening *all* the presents."

Erik throws a t-shirt on and we head upstairs to where my boy is bouncing around the tree. He sees me and screams, "Mommy, *look!* Santa was here!" Grant points to the empty plate and empty glass, and then points to the presents.

"I see that, baby. Merry Christmas!" He runs to me, and I pick him up, kissing all over his face.

Gretchen comes down in an outfit similar to mine, and the rest of the adults start coming down. Grant hasn't moved from his spot next to the tree as he looks at each wrapped gift with rapt attention.

It takes us about ten minutes to get coffee and throw breakfast in the oven. Then we all gather in the living room. We're letting Grant open his Santa presents before we eat breakfast and we'll open the rest after.

We all sit and watch as Grant sits on Gretchen's lap and opens gift after gift. My heart is so full as I listen to his excited glee as he opens each gift. My boy loves everything, and as I look around, everyone smiles as they watch him.

Once he's finished, we head into the dining room for breakfast. Everyone chatters happily as they eat, and I just take it all in. I don't even think when things were good with my parents that we were talkative like Erik's family is. Gretchen and Grant finish eating first, and she takes him to get washed up so we can get breakfast cleared and head out to the living room.

Curled up next to Erik, I watch everyone open gifts. I've got a pile in front of me, but I'm enjoying watching the others. Gretchen loved her snow globe from Grant, and she'd gotten him the *Jurassic Park* movies, because he's got a love for dinosaurs. Most fourteen-year-olds wouldn't want a five-year-old hanging on them, but the petite blonde just smiles and does whatever my boy wants.

Erik's parents were thrilled with their gifts, and Nicole actually cried when she opened her bracelet. I had no clue what to get for Erik—he's not a high-maintenance guy, so I just got him some t-shirts, and this cool USMC picture. I sit and watch nervously as he opens the picture.

He turns to me. "I love it. Thank you."

I realize they're all waiting on me to open my presents. I got a pretty sweater and scarf from his mom and dad, and Gretchen got me a couple of bath bombs. I thank them for the gifts even though a teeny tiny part of me is kind of hurt that Erik didn't get me anything, but the hurt goes away when I sit back and Erik places a familiar blue box on my lap.

My hands tremble as I pull the lid off. A gasp leaves my lips and tears fill my eyes. It's a platinum chain with a pendant on it with the letter G and Grant's birthstone. "Do you like it?"

I know we're in front of his family but I crawl into his lap, burying my face in his neck. "It's the most beautiful thing I've ever seen. Thank you so much."

I get off his lap, and he puts my necklace on for me. I put my hand over it, taking a deep breath. I really don't want to cry in front of his family, but one tear manages to escape.

Grant comes over to me. "It's pretty, Mommy. Look it's a G, for Grant."

I wrap my arms around him. "Or G for Grunt." I tickle his sides until he's squealing.

After we finish our coffee, I help Nicole clean up the mess we made unwrapping presents. Everyone else appears to be in some sort of Nerf gun battle. It's comical to watch grown-ass men crawl around on the floor, hide in closets, and shoot each other with the orange darts.

Gretchen disappears upstairs to call her friends— to tell them about her gifts, no doubt. Once the mess is cleaned up, Nicole and I sit at the breakfast bar and drink the last of the coffee.

"Why don't you see your parents?" My eyes widen, and she sees it. "I'm sorry, that was rude and none of my business."

I grab her hand. "N-No, it's okay. It's not the easiest thing to talk about, but we were never super close. After being around your family, I see that now. I think that's why it was so easy for them to turn their back on me when I refused to leave my abusive ex. Even after I left, they didn't want anything to do with me." I wipe away the lone tear that falls. "Ugh, sorry for being a downer."

"Oh honey, you're not a downer. I'm sorry I made you feel like you had to tell me." Nicole gives me a hug, and when I pull back, she looks closer at my necklace. "My boy did good."

I nod. "He did. I love it so much." Arms wrap around me, and I tilt my head back, looking up at Erik. "Best. Gift. Ever." I smile up at him.

"Will you be okay here for a little bit? Mom and I are going to take a wreath to dad's grave today. We won't be gone very long."

"No, of course, go. We'll be fine."

They leave shortly after. While they're gone, the rest of us lounge in the living room watching *A Christmas Story*.

CHAPTER FIFTEEN

Erik

It's been over two weeks since Christmas, and there's been no activity at Shayla's apartment. Last week she'd asked about Grant and her returning home, but I changed the subject. The truth is I don't *want* them to leave—I love having them in my space even though I seriously never in a million years would've thought I'd want to be domesticated. They make it so easy to want to be with them all the time. Even their damn furball, who seems to love me, has grown on me.

I sit down in the conference room waiting for the others to arrive for our monthly staff meeting, which is just us talking about the cases we're working on and bouncing ideas around. Plus it gives us a chance to catch up. Jack used to have us meet for weekly dinners, but we seem to keep getting busier and busier, so those dinners have been getting further and further apart.

Reece and Marcus walk in and take their seats around the table. "How was Charlie's first

162

Christmas?" I ask.

The proud papa pulls out his phone and shows me tons of pictures he's taken of her. In one, she's in a sleeper that says, "Baby's First Christmas" with her eyes closed. In the next, she's lying on a blanket under the Christmas tree…sleeping. In yet *another* picture, she's in a little green dress and leggings, and Del's holding her…Charlie's out like a light.

"Dude, your daughter is lazy." I smile as I hand his phone back to him. Marcus snickers from beside me.

"Fuck you, she's not lazy. She's amazing, and I'm going to teach her to always spit up on her Uncle Erik." We've all claimed the title of "uncle" for Charlie and Leif.

I shake my head. "Never gonna happen—I'm too good-looking. She plans on saving that for her dad because he's an ugly motherfucker."

"Both of you ain't got nothing on me," Marcus announces. "Uncle Marcus is going to be the favorite." We both look at him and roll our eyes.

Once everyone gets here, we go around the room discussing each case. In the middle of the meeting, Marcus gets a call about a skip that he needs to hunt down.

When we finish up, I head to Shayla's temporary office. The door is open, and there are a dozen pink roses sitting on her desk. I know I shouldn't, but I'm fucking nosy and look for a card, but I don't see one.

I step out as Shayla comes out of the bathroom. Her face lights up when she sees me, and I don't miss that she's wearing the necklace I got her for

Christmas. She comes up to me and wraps her arms around my waist. "How did you know that pink roses are my favorite flower?"

My stomach dips, and I don't like it. "Baby, I didn't send them to you."

Her face pales, and she walks past me into the office—I follow her. "Don't touch them," I warn. "Just in case we need to dust the vase for prints. I'll be right back."

I head out front to talk to Carrie. "The flowers that came for Shayla—do you know the name of the florist?"

She looks confused. "You didn't send them?"

"No, I didn't, and there's no card."

Carrie always keeps a copy of whatever she signs just in case there's ever a need, like now, to trace the origin of a delivery. Maybe we're all just very untrusting. She pulls out the folder and grabs me the piece of paper with the name of the florist on it. It's the one just down the street from us. "I'll be right back," I tell her before I take the stairs down to the main floor. I quickly reach Julia's Flower Boutique and I'm immediately nauseated by the overpowering floral scents.

At the counter, an older woman glances up at me. "Can I help you?"

Time to lay on the charm. "I sure hope you can. We had some beautiful roses delivered to our office, but they didn't come with a card. I was hoping you could help me out and let me know who sent them."

"What type of flowers?"

"Pink roses in a glass vase, and they were delivered to one of our staff, named Shayla Martin, over at Rogue Security and Investigation." I lean against the counter and give her my signature smile.

She peers at me over the rims of her glasses. "I can't give you that information, and I wasn't here when the order was placed."

Damn. "Okay, thanks." I head back to the office and to Shayla's desk.

When she sees me, she stands up. "Did you find out anything?"

"No—she wouldn't give me any information. Do you think maybe it was your parents?" She shakes her head. "Your brother?"

"I don't think they even know where I am. What if it's Ryan? He brought me pink roses on our first date. Those were the flowers that I had when we were married." Her voice is whisper soft.

I stop right in front of her, grabbing her shoulders. "How could it be? You haven't heard from him in two years. How would he even know where to look? There's been no activity at your place, either. Just sit tight; let me go talk to the guys." She nods, and I bend down, kissing her lips. "It's going to be okay."

I leave her and head down to the conference room, and thankfully find Jack, Coby, and Reece still sitting around the table. "What's up, Erik?" Jack asks as I shut the door.

I don't sugarcoat it. "I need to find someone," I grit out. "Shayla's ex-husband used to beat her." The moment the words leave my lips, I can feel the air charge. "She left him and pressed charges after he hit her and Grant walked in on it. The fucker only served six months since it was the one and only time she ever reported the abuse to the police. She hasn't seen him since, but today someone anonymously sent her pink roses. They're her favorite flower, and she carried pink roses on her wedding day."

"I'm on it," Coby speaks up. "Just give me any information that I need, and I'll start looking for him."

I write down everything I know. "Thanks, man. I owe you, especially if I can find the fucking woman beater piece of shit."

Coby's young, but fucking smart and a bulldog. He disappears out of the conference room, and I know he's going to get started looking for the asshole right away.

Reece shakes his head. "I don't understand how any man can hurt a woman…and why does trouble seem to follow the women in our lives?" He looks at me. "Whatever you need from me, just holler."

"Thanks, brother." We may have only known each other a short time, but Reece's become so much more than a co-worker—okay, that makes us sound like we're a couple. But we've bonded, and we all went through Delilah's ordeal right along with him.

Reece stands up and leaves; now it's just Jack and me. "How worried are you about this guy coming back into her life?" he asks.

"I honestly don't know. There's no sign he's been near her place." I lean forward in my chair. "What do you think?"

"I don't know, but we should assume it's him. The bigger question is: Why? It's been two years. If he was looking for revenge or payback, he wouldn't have waited this long." We both stand up. "Use whatever resources we've got. I'd rather be overly cautious. I don't want to be surprised ever again."

I clap my hand on his shoulder. "Thanks, Jack. I can't let anything happen to them."

"We'll make fucking sure that doesn't happen. Let me know if I can help with anything." He follows me out of the conference room.

Jack heads into his office, and I stop in Shayla's. "Hey, baby." I hate the spooked look on her face. "It's going to be okay. We're all over it." She nods, although it's not very convincing.

I kiss her before heading back to my office. No matter what, I'll do whatever it takes to protect her and Grant—I protect what's mine.

***

"Fuck, baby. Ride me harder." I grip Shayla's hips so tightly that I know I'll be leaving marks on her, but that just makes my dick harder. She bites her lip to muffle her moan as I reach down farther and grab two handfuls of juicy ass cheek. I bend my knees just enough that she settles deep on my cock. Her pussy flutters around me, and I can feel her arousal running down my balls.

Shayla grabs onto my shoulders, and I situate her legs so her feet are resting on the mattress on both sides of my hips. "I need to come," she moans.

"Tell me how bad you need to come, Shayla," I whisper against her throat.

She bites her lip and looks down before looking

back up at him. "*Please* make me come. I ache so bad it hurts. Don't make me wait."

Grabbing her tits, I squeeze one nipple and then suck the other into my mouth. Her nipples are so sensitive she can almost come just from stimulation of them alone. Shayla begins rolling her hips as she bounces up down. Seriously, best sex ever. I can make her fall apart with barely a touch.

Her moves become erratic as I can feel her begin to come. "Give me your lips," I moan as I remove my mouth from her breast. Shayla leans down and moans against my lips as I feel her come over and over. I grab her hips, pinning her down as I thrust up, coming so hard I see stars.

I pull my softening cock from her pussy, and I love the sleepy whimper that leaves her lips. Leaving her for only a minute, I go into the bathroom to clean up and take a leak.

Back in our bedroom, Shayla is burrowed under the blankets—she's always cold. "Did you check on Grant?" I ask her as I slide into bed.

"Passed out and snoring." She scooches into my side.

Wrapping my arms around her, I kiss her forehead.

Just before she falls asleep, I swear I hear her mumble, "I love you."

Too bad she's already asleep when I whisper back, "I love you too."

***

Today is a true test on how much headway I'm

making with Grant. Shayla is going to dinner with Carrie at Delilah's house, so I told her I'd pick up Grant from Luna's and feed him dinner. He's opened up a lot to me, but I want him to know I'm a good guy who cares about his mother.

Luna answers the door right away. "Hi, Erik. Shayla said you were coming to get Grunt." She turns toward the hall and hollers, "Grunt, Erik's here to get you."

That sweet boy runs toward me. "Hi, Erik." It surprises me even more when he hugs my legs. "Can we have pizza?" The kid could eat pizza all day every day, and he'd be completely fine with that.

"Do you want to go to the place by mine?"

He nods, and I help him get his coat, hat, and gloves on before we say goodbye and leave. Grant's quiet at first, but then he starts asking me questions. "Where's Mommy? When will she be home? Is she going to tuck me in?"

"Remember? Mommy is with Carrie and Delilah. If she's not home by the time you go to bed, I'll make sure she comes in and kisses you. Does that sound okay?" I glance back in the rearview mirror and see Grant smile at me and nod.

We pull up in front of Gino's and run in to grab our pizza and a four pack of deluxe root beer. When we get home, I feed the cat quickly before we sit down to eat. During dinner, Grant's pretty quiet, but that's because the kid is *really* serious when it comes to his food. The root beer I bought is in bottles, so he thinks he's a big boy.

After we eat, I get his bath ready. Shayla said

that I only needed to help him with washing his hair and making sure he gets all the soap out. Not knowing what the rules are, I turn my back while he strips out of his clothes and then climbs into the tub. I put soap on his little washcloth, and he starts scrubbing his body.

"Make sure you get all the nooks and crannies," I tell him.

He looks at me with those big brown eyes—just like his mom's. "What's a cranny?"

"Uh…I'm not exactly sure, but I'm sure it means every little part of your body. In other words, wash everything." He must understand that, because he stands up and does a really thorough job of scrubbing himself down.

Once he's done, I wash his hair and rinse it before letting him play until his hands are little prunes. I comb his hair back and have him change into his pajamas. When we get settled on the couch, I turn on *Jurassic Park*. He surprises me when he scoots in next to me, leaning into my side.

He's sound asleep by the time all hell breaks loose in the park. I should shut the movie off and do some work, but I forgot how fun these films are. I lie down on the couch with him lying in front of me, and that's how Shayla finds us when she gets home.

"Hi, how was he?" she whispers.

"He was perfect. He's a good kid. We had pizza and drank root beer out of the bottle." I grab my phone and show her the picture of Grant sitting at the table with his pizza and bottle of root beer.

"Oh my gosh, this is so cute." I take my phone back and stand up, bringing him with me.

We get him settled and then head back into the living room. "How was dinner?" I ask her.

"It was good. We had both Charlie and Leif, so there was *lots* of baby snuggling. It was nice, and it was great to get to know them both better. Egan stayed out front when they dropped me off until he knew I was on the elevator."

We've been a little more watchful this past week with Shayla. Nothing's happened, but we're not taking any chances—*I'm* not taking any chances. She curls up with her Kindle against me while I finish the movie because, yes, I'm watching *Jurassic Park* by myself and not apologetic about it.

Shayla starts nodding off so I send her to bed, telling her I'll be in after the news.

CHAPTER SIXTEEN

Shayla

I stare at the pictures on my phone, and I feel a mixture of anger and sadness. Erik's been out of the office a lot this week. He's had a couple of cases he's been working on, which have had him running all over Chicago.

This morning had started like any other day. Erik woke me with his tongue between my legs until I came. We're not using condoms anymore, so he slid inside of me with a groan and fucked me nice and slowly until I came again and he followed not far behind. We took a shower, and then I got Grant up and ready to go to Luna's.

We dropped him off, and then Erik dropped me off at the office. I've been busy all morning, checking everyone's licenses to make sure they're not close to expiring and ordering more security equipment for Egan.

The first text came about an hour ago.

Unknown: How does it feel to know that you

can't please anyone?

At first I thought it was the wrong number so I ignored it, but then two more texts came.

Unknown: You're pathetic, and you've always been pathetic.

Unknown: That new boyfriend of yours sure has women hanging off his dick, I wonder if he's banging one of them right now.

My stomach starts to turn, but I'm not letting someone I don't know intimidate me.

Shayla: I think you're texting the wrong person.

The dots begin to dance, and nausea swirls in my belly.

Unknown: Oh you dumb bitch, I'm most definitely not texting the wrong person....Shayla.

Tears burn my eyes. It *has* to be Ryan, and if it is, what does he know? My phone dings a few more times, but I don't dare look right now because I'm terrified of what I might see.

What if Erik's just like Ryan? Sure, he'd never hit me, but what if he's cheating on me? He's admitted he's never had a real relationship before. Maybe this is just too much for him. I mean, he

173

went from being single and playing the field to being in a relationship with a single mom.

I grab my phone and open up Messenger. The first picture is a close-up of Erik's face, and he's wearing that cocky grin of his. The second picture is him in a Starbucks, leaning against the counter talking to the girl behind the counter. It's not hard to miss the way her eyes are bright and her smile is shy.

The other two photos are much the same: He's giving a woman his signature smile, and she's leaning into him like she can't help herself. But it's the last picture that has me feeling truly sick. He's sitting with a gorgeous, leggy blonde, and he's leaning in so close it looks like they're about to kiss.

I *have* to get out of here—I can't be here anymore. I grab all of my stuff off Delilah's desk and shove it into my bag. Luckily, it's just a few pictures—of course I leave the one picture of Erik, Grant, and me because I'm a delusional idiot. How did I ever think he'd be into someone like me?

I'll call Delilah later and let her know that I'm quitting, once I calm down. I love working here, but if he's really played me for a fool, then I can't stay. Everyone would be like, "That poor, stupid woman."

I quickly shut down my laptop, grab my coat and bag, and head out. I need to be quick—the fewer people to see me leave, the better. Unfortunately, Carrie is sitting behind her desk. "Shay? What's wrong? Where are you going?"

Instead of answering her, I make my way toward

the stairs and head down. On quick feet, I make my way toward the Blue Line and stick my earbuds in while I wait. I dig inside my bag for my phone, but I don't find it. "Shit," I whisper. I suppose I'll just have to get a new one.

What if I'm making a mistake? My eyes burn, and my chest aches. I just want things to go back to the way they were this morning, not now when suddenly all my old insecurities are rushing back.

I get off at my stop and walk the three blocks to my apartment. I'm ready for spring; I am *so* sick of the cold already. I reach my street and head up to Luna and Rocco's place. It's time to put on an act so they don't suspect something is wrong, because honestly, I don't know for sure if there *is* something wrong.

When I knock, Rocco opens the door. "Hey, come on in. The kids are reading." Sure enough, all three kids are sitting around the living room with books in their hands. Once Grant sees I'm here, he puts his book down. While he's getting his coat on, Luna comes out and gives me a hug.

When we head down the stairs, he looks at me with a confused expression. "Where's Erik, Mommy?"

"Umm…he's working. I just thought it might be nice to stay here. We can have some macaroni and cheese." That seems to appease him as we step inside. It's cold and smells a little musty—after I turn the heat up, I open a couple of windows. While Grant sits on the couch watching TV, I quickly dust every surface that's covered in the stuff.

While I get the water going, I lean against the

counter and lower my head. I wish I had my phone, but then maybe it's good I don't. I don't want to see those pictures ever again.

***

Erik

The minute I step off the elevator, I realize something's wrong. Carrie's behind her desk looking troubled. "What's up? What's going on?" I step close to her desk.

"Egan needs to see you."

I open the doors to the back and make my way toward Egan's space. I give a knock and open the door. Egan's watching the screen. "What's going on, man?"

"About an hour and a half ago, Carrie came back to let me know that Shayla left urgently, and wouldn't answer when she called her, but then we realized it was because she must've forgotten her phone because it was sitting on her desk." He hands me her phone. "I *may* have hacked it since it was locked. Look at the text messages. We didn't want to look, but it was like something spooked her."

I open her messages. "That *motherfucker*!" I growl. Every picture was taken just right to make me look bad. I read what that piece of shit said to her before he sent the pictures—it's *got* to be her ex. He knew *exactly* what to say to her and what to send to get a reaction from her.

"She's in her apartment, and they're okay, but she's freaking out," Egan says. "You can see whatever mental war she's fighting all over her face." I sit down and stare at the screen. She's leaning against the counter and staring at the camera. When they'd been installed, I showed her where they were all placed.

Shayla moves to a drawer, and I watch her pull out paper and start writing. When she's done, she walks to the counter and holds the sign up.

Can someone call Erik? I need him.

I'm out the door without a second thought. I drive a little faster than I should, but I need to get to her. I have no clue what's going through her mind right now. It takes me thirty minutes to get to her place due to traffic. I find a spot down the street, hop out, and rush toward her apartment.

Shayla's standing in the doorway when I reach her, and she begins to cry. I scoop her up in my arms and hug her tight to my chest. "It's okay, baby. I'm here."

"I'm sorry I even let those thoughts enter my mind. He just-just wanted to hurt me." She buries her face in my neck. "I should've called you instead of assuming the worst."

I set her down on her feet and cup her face. "It's okay."

"Erik!" I'm pleasantly surprised when Grant comes running toward me. I pick him up and he wraps his arms around my neck. "Mommy said you were working late. Are we going home now?"

"Yeah buddy, we're going home." God, that sounds so fucking good to say. "Do you need to do anything?" I ask her. I reach into my coat pocket and pull out her cell phone. "And here, Egan kept this for you."

"Thanks. I just need to clean up dishes from dinner, and then I need to make a call."

I put Grant's coat on. "Sit right here, bud. I'll be right back." In the kitchen, Shayla's scrubbing the dishes and quickly putting them in the dish rack. She grabs her phone off the counter, pushes a couple of buttons, and then holds it to her ear.

"You son of a bitch—how *dare* you try and weasel your way back into our lives—" I snatch the phone away from her. "*Hey*, I wasn't done."

"I know, baby, but don't sink to that fucker's level. We don't know what his end game is, and we don't want to provoke him."

She nods. "I just wanted him to know that he isn't going to come between us."

"Let's get out of here. You know we should talk about upgrading to a bigger place." I throw that out there—might as well. She just stares at me. I know she had a little drama earlier, but I *know* what I want.

"Are you serious?" she asks. "Don't you think it's too soon? Plus, what if Ryan starts messing with me?"

"As long as I live, I will *not* let him get anywhere near either of you." I hope she can hear the conviction in my voice, because I mean it.

"Okay. I won't call him again." I wrap my arms around her, hugging her to my chest.

We lock up, and then get Grant loaded into my Explorer before heading home. Shayla's quiet on the ride back and stares out the passenger-side window. I'm giving her the space she needs for now, but tonight once Grant's asleep, we should talk. I should explain the pictures to her. I want to knock out any little kernel of doubt that might be still swirling around in her head.

She needs to know that I'd never cheat on her. Even when I played the field I never made promises or let the women I took to bed think there was anything more between us than a casual thing.

We get home, and I carry Grant inside. I set him down in the elevator and let him push the button for our floor. Once inside, Grant grabs Lucifer and takes him back into his bedroom. I hang up my coat, and then Shayla's, in the closet. In our bedroom, I find Shayla sitting on the end of the bed and she's looking at her phone.

I get close and look down—she's looking at the pictures he sent her. I don't even know this stupid fuck, but I fucking hate him.

Sitting down next to her, I take the phone from her hands. "I want to explain what these pictures are. It's no question that I've fallen for you hard—I don't want you to feel any doubts about us at all." I scrub my face with my hands. "Yes, I've heavily flirted with women to get them to tell me stuff. I know it makes me sound like a shitty person, but sometimes we have to do what we have to do to get information." I turn to look at her, and she's staring at her hands.

"Baby, I've never fucked someone for information. Yeah, I've flirted—*heavily*, but I'm not that big of a dick to cross that line." I've come *close* to crossing it, but I couldn't do it. "I would *never* cheat on you. I know you have no reason to believe me, but if it's any consolation, you're it for me. You and Grant mean so much to me."

She reaches out, laces her fingers through mine, and then rests her head on my shoulder. Grant comes in and climbs up on my lap. "Can I have a snack?"

I kiss Shayla's forehead and stand up with Grant in my arms. "How about I slice up an apple with some peanut butter?"

"That sounds yummy." In such a short amount of time, this little boy has wormed his way into my heart. At first he wouldn't even acknowledge me, and now we've bonded.

In the kitchen I have him sit down at the breakfast bar while I slice his apple, putting it on a plate with glob of peanut butter. In no time, Grant's plate is empty and he's licking the peanut butter off. "Okay, dude. I think you got it all."

"Erik, how did your arms get so big?" He looks at me curiously.

"Come on, I'll show you what I do." I pick him up and set him on the ground. He follows me into the living room, where I get down on the floor. He watches me as I start doing pushups and then starts copying me. Up and down, we move together; I'm not even breaking a sweat, but I see his little arms shake as he keeps going.

When we stop, I smile when I see Shayla watching us from the mouth of the hall. "Mommy, did you see me? I'm gonna have big muscles like Erik." He jumps up and down, his excitement palpable. Grant flexes for us, showing us his "muscles." We do some crunches while Shayla continues to watch.

Then he sits on my back while I do some more pushups. His giggle is contagious as I go up and down with him on my back. I roll over on my back when he gets off and then grab him again and do some bench presses and curls.

Shayla's cell phone rings and I hop up, looking at her caller ID. "Give it to me?" She reluctantly hands it over. I take it down the hall to my room before I answer. "What?"

"Well, well, well. This must be the guy that's trying to steal my family."

I roll my eyes. This guy is a complete moron. "Dude, they haven't been yours since the first time you struck her."

"All I was trying to do was train her to be the type of wife that I wanted. It's not my fault that she wouldn't listen to me. She needed lots of lessons." This guy is a real big fucking tool, and I really hope he shows his face so I can plant my fist into it.

"Listen fuckface, I don't know what you were trying to do by sending those pictures to her, but she knows I'm not you, and I don't need to stick my dick in any available female to prove that I'm a real man." I disconnect the call and block his number.

I look up and find Shayla watching me from the doorway. When I hold my hand out to her, she walks hesitantly toward me and takes my hand. I wrap my arms around her waist, resting my forehead against her stomach. A sigh slips past my lips when I feel her fingers run through my hair.

"I've never wanted to put my fist in someone's face more," I murmur.

"I'm so sorry, Erik."

I hug her tighter. "You have nothing to be sorry for."

"I just don't know why he's messing with us all of a sudden," she says quietly.

"Baby, guys like that...there's no rhyme or reason for why they do the things they do, but my guess he's been on probation and didn't want to screw that up." Tilting my head back, I look up at her. "I'm not going to let anything happen to you— *or* to Grant."

CHAPTER SEVENTEEN

Shayla

Everyone's been so sweet to me since I walked into the office with Erik earlier. A part of me wanted to just take today off, but I couldn't do that to Carrie. When she saw me step out of the elevator she rushed me and gave me a hug. *That* was all I needed.

I don't have a ton of work to get caught up on, but that's because I've worked my butt off this morning to make sure whatever I was working on before I left got finished first. I'm in the middle of checking emails when Jack stops by my office.

"How are you doing?" He sits down across from me. The man is huge and intimidating, but he has an equally huge heart that makes him slightly less intimidating whenever he smiles or talks about his granddaughter.

"I'm good. I'm sorry I left the way I did. That wasn't very professional." I look down at my lap, slightly embarrassed that I behaved the way I did.

"Don't be sorry." I look up at him. "Tell me

183

about your ex." He's not asking, but at least now I no longer feel shame when I talk about my marriage.

While I tell him everything, he sits and listens without saying a word, but I can feel the anger coming off him in waves. I'm not sure if it's just from me working with all these alpha males for so long, but their moods are palpable now—more so when they're pissed off.

By the time I'm done, I feel embarrassed all over again. When will that feeling end?

"Sweetheart, don't get embarrassed; I can see it on your face that you are. Sometimes we're blinded by love, or lust, and it makes it hard for us to see the truth. After all the shit with Del's mom, I felt like such an idiot because I didn't see what she was truly capable of. Because of her and her actions I almost lost not only my daughter, but my granddaughter too. They're narcissists with a little sociopath in them. It's nothing we did, except to be manipulated."

We talk a little longer, and he shows me some pictures on his phone of little Charlie before he heads out.

When I finish my work for the day, I stay right where I am per Erik's orders. I know he's going to be more protective of me, but I'm okay with that. Luna and Rocco were told about the situation and were given the choice if they still wanted to watch Grant, or if I should bring him to work, which Jack was fine with if that kept my son safe. Luna and Rocco chose to keep Grant with them.

They know how to get ahold of us at the office,

and I showed her the one photo I have of Ryan so they'll know what he looks like. When Erik looked over my shoulder and saw the picture his body stiffened and he got real pissed. I still don't know why, but I'm sure he'll tell me eventually.

While I sit in the break room, Dalton comes in and takes a seat across from me. I love Dalton— he's so funny, but you can see the hint of badass swirling beneath the surface. "How are you doing, love?"

"I'm okay, just waiting for Erik to pick me up. What are you doing here so late?" He teaches self-defense classes, especially in areas with higher crime rates.

"I had to talk to Jack." He leans into the table. "You know, if you want, I can teach you some self-defense. Nothing too fancy, but enough to disable them, and to give you time to get away from your assailant."

"That might be a good idea, thanks. Do you think maybe you could teach Grant some stuff? I mean, I know he's only five, but I figure there might be some moves that it'd be good if he learned."

"Absolutely. I'll talk to Erik and have him bring you guys to my gym. It should only take a couple of hours."

I stand up to hug him goodbye and tell him that I'm looking forward to learning some moves. My phone rings, and my stomach knots when I grab it out of my bag. I relax when I remember that Erik blocked Ryan's number. "Hello?"

"Ms. Martin, this is Gregory downstairs, and Mr.

Walker is pulling up in about five minutes. He has asked for you to wait downstairs for him. I'm to keep you behind the desk with me until he arrives."

"Oh okay, sure. I'll be right down." I gather my things, put my coat on, and head for the elevator. As I wait, a small smile graces my lips when I think about learning some self-defense moves…and using them on Erik.

When the doors slide open and I step on, in a flash a hand wraps around my throat and my back hits the wall. I stare into the cold, beady eyes of my ex-husband. I grab onto his wrist, trying to pull it off. But he's not choking me—he's just using the move that he always used to when he had a point to make.

"W-What do you want, Ryan?" I croak. "Can't you just leave me alone? We're divorced…you have no claim to me anymore."

"Oh baby, we're *just* getting started." The elevator doors open, he lets me go, and I sag against the wall. I shouldn't have let my guard down, because I don't see the fist hitting me in the stomach until it's too late.

My breath leaves me in a wheeze, and I hit my knees just as he steps off. The doors slide shut. When the cab finally opens up to the lobby, I stumble out and right into Erik. "Baby, what the fuck!"

He lifts me up into his arms and carries me back onto the elevator. When it lets us off on the Rogue floor, we're greeted by the man on the team, Josh, who watches the monitors until morning. "*Shit*, Erik, I watched him grab her, but he was already

186

gone by the time we made our way down to the floor where he got off."

"Thanks, man." Josh heads into the back and leaves us alone.

My breathing starts to even out and I place a hand against my stomach. "Baby, tell me what happened," Erik asks.

"I...I was waiting for you in the break room, and my phone rang. When I answered it, he said he was Gregory from downstairs, and that you told him to have me meet you downstairs. As soon as I stepped onto the elevator, he grabbed me by the throat. I asked him why he was doing this, and he said he was j-just getting started. When the doors opened he let me go, but then he p-punched me in the stomach." I feel so ashamed I fell for Ryan's tricks.

Of course, during our marriage he'd be sweet enough to get me to let my guard down and then he'd strike, quick like a snake. "I'm *so* sorry, Erik. I shouldn't have gone downstairs."

"It's okay, but baby...no more, okay? If it's not me or one of my team talking—and I'll program their numbers into your phone—then you're to stay right where you're at and call me."

I nod. "Yes, I promise I won't go anywhere unless it's you telling me to do it."

He wraps his arms around me and kisses the top of my head. "Let's get Grant and go home."

***

"Brilliant, Grant!" Dalton pats my son on the back. "Let's do it again." I watch Dalton grab for

187

Grant, and my boy lets his body go limp and then kicks at Dalton's leg. I clap when Grant hops back up and runs around Dalton.

Erik sits next to me, and he's been shouting encouraging words at Grant while Dalton flips him around the mat. Of course he was just as vocal while I was flipped around like I weighed nothing, and was shown some moves to get away if someone were to grab me. The best was when Erik got up and tussled with me, which was fun and a huge turn-on.

After we finish, we head back home to get cleaned up. Lucifer meets us at the door. "Hi, baby." I pick up my fat cat and hold him to my chest. He's definitely made himself at home and doesn't seem to be destroying any of Erik's stuff, thank goodness.

When I step out of the shower, I hear Erik's voice. "Mom, I don't know if that's a good idea right now." A pause. "Yes, I know he'd have a good time, but Shayla's ex is being a pain in the ass." Another pause. "Okay, let me talk it over with Shayla."

I step into the bedroom, and he holds his hand out to me. "Do your parents want to keep Grant?"

I sit on his lap, wrapped in my towel. "Yeah, Gretchen wants to see him, and I didn't think it was a good idea for her to come here, so she wants Grant to come stay with them. I just don't know if that's a good idea, either." I wrap my arms around him. "Marcus has family not far from there, so maybe he can hang out a bit. He knows my mom, Tad, and Gretchen."

"Well, I'll leave it up to you. As long as you think he's safe, then I'm fine with whatever it is you want to do."

He leaves me to get dressed and start lunch. I take a moment to sit on his bed—correction, *our* bed—wrap my hand around the pendant on the necklace he bought for me, and thank the powers that be for bringing him into my life.

After lunch, I lie down for a nap but can't sleep. My mind just whirls with all the shit that Ryan has pulled. I want answers. I want to know: *Why?* What did I ever do to him except love him? I tried to give him a good home, and a son. *He's* the one who pissed it away, and it took me a long time to realize that it wasn't my fault.

I'm strong now. For Grant I had to be, and will continue to be. I peek out into the hall and can hear a movie playing in the other room. Grabbing my phone, I go into Erik's closet so he can't hear me talking.

I pull up Ryan's number and hit send. It rings twice before he answers. "I knew you'd call me sooner or later. I'll think about taking you back, but you're going to have to work for it."

I don't answer at first because I'm stunned. He thinks I really going to go back to him, that I would expose our son to that? Ryan has seriously not asked about our son—I mean *my* son—at all.

"Shayla," he snaps.

"Oh no, you're *not* going to talk to me like that. How dare you send me roses, try to jeopardize my relationship with a wonderful man, and how dare you fucking *threaten me*. I used to be so frightened

189

of you, but now I realize I should pity you, you fucking piece of woman-beating shit. I hope while you were in jail that you were someone's bitch." I disconnect the call and realize my hands are shaking.

I open the closet door and find Erik sitting on the end of his bed. Shit, he looks pissed. I'm tempted to go back into the closet, but I don't. "Erik, listen before you say—" He holds up his hand. "Erik, please, I'm—"

"Shayla, shut the fuck up." I snap my mouth shut. "What did I tell you? I told you we didn't know what his end game was. We also don't want to provoke him. You just said that when he was in jail you hope he was someone's bitch." His lip twitches, and I feel myself relax…a little. "Come here, mouthy." I crawl onto his lap. "I love that sassy little mouth of yours. When Grunt goes to bed, I'm going to fuck it." He rubs his thumb along my lower lip.

"Seriously though, I'm so fucking happy that you're not letting him hurt you anymore, but someone who's clearly unstable shouldn't be provoked. If he's capable of hurting you, there's no telling what he could do. Promise me that if you're feeling impulsive, you'll let me know. You can just use that sassy mouth on me instead."

I kiss his cheek. "I promise that I won't call him again. I just wish he'd disappear. It's like we're going to have to look over our shoulders until we know what he's up to."

Erik's arms tighten around me for a moment. "I'm working on that. Just trust me, okay?"

I nod because I *do* trust him, and have to trust that he's got my and Grant's best interests at heart.

Grant rushes into the room. "What are you guys doing? You're missing the dinosaurs." He then holds up his hands like claws and roars.

Erik moves me off his lap and holds up his hands like claws. He does some weird half-growl and half-roar before chasing Grant out of the bedroom. My son's giggles melt my heart, and I can barely stand it.

I get up and head out into the living room. Erik is on his back on the floor and is bench pressing Grant while he watches one of the *Jurassic Park* movies. I think those are his favorite gifts; he's been through the entire film series twice. It's about the only time he holds still for an extended length of time.

They don't notice me at first, so I just sit in the corner of the couch watching them, and my heart is full. I'll be damned if I let Ryan take this away from me.

***

My tongue swirls around the head of his cock, and it makes me wet to hear him moan like he is. I swallow him down as far as I can, and when I drag my tongue up the underside while I cup his balls in my hand, he grips my hair in a punishing grip. Up and down, I suck him into my mouth. "Fuck baby, use that sassy fucking mouth. *Fuuuccck*!"

I hold his cock at the base as I suck him with all I've got. Every few sucks, I let my tongue swirl around the purple crown. His balls tighten in my hand, and I know that he's so close to coming. Increasing my suction, I bob up and down.

"I'm going to come, baby. Let go or I'm going to come in that sassy mouth of yours." Instead of pulling off his dick, I keep up my suction until that first splash of cum hits my tongue. I swallow every drop, moaning as the salty, viscous fluid flows down my throat.

Erik pulls me off his softening cock with a pop and guides me up until I'm straddling his face. I try to push myself off him because I've never done oral this way and I'm self-conscious, but before I can, he spears me with his tongue. Gripping the headboard, I moan as he begins to work my pussy over.

When he sucks my clit into his mouth and then nips it with his teeth, I have to cover my mouth to keep from crying out. When the ripples stop, he pulls me into his arms and kisses me. I taste myself on his tongue, and it makes me moan into his mouth.

He pulls his mouth away from mine. "I'm in love with you, Shayla." I freeze, stunned speechless—my eyes begin to burn. I've never heard such beautiful words, but they scare me. Ryan was my *husband* and I never heard him say those words to me.

Like a damn fish, my mouth opens and closes, but nothing comes out. I want nothing more than to tell him that I'm in love with him too, but I'm scared.

Erik reaches out and strokes my cheek. "You don't need to say it. I just wanted you to know that I do."

A tear leaks from my eye, and Erik pulls me toward him. All he does is hold me as I cry silent tears because I have this amazing man who loves me and loves my son. He hasn't said it, but I can tell. I hate that Ryan broke that part inside of me.

CHAPTER EIGHTEEN

Erik

I slip the cover off my Impala, eager for nicer weather so I can drive this beast around. Grant would get a kick out of riding in my baby, especially the way it rumbles when I turn her on. I'd love to get Shayla in this baby, and go parking. My dick twitches with just the thought of burying myself in her pussy.

Since we've stopped using condoms I can't get enough of her, but a teeny tiny part of me in the last week has started thinking about watching her belly grow with my baby planted in there. I haven't shared that with Shayla because I don't want to send her running as far as possible from me. I shake off those thoughts or I'll end up heading back to the office and taking Shayla against the wall in her office.

I climb in the driver's side and stick the key in the ignition. It takes a couple of tries before my baby roars to life. I rest the back of my head on the seat and just listen to her purr. Ten minutes later I turn her off, lock her up, and put the cover back on.

Reece pulls into the garage directly behind my Impala. His Mustang is a thing of beauty. "What's up, brother?" We give each other the half handshake, half backslap bullshit.

"Not much, man—how are your girls?" The fool always smiles like a crazy person when you bring up his family.

"They're amazing. I swear when Charlie hears my voice she looks for me." He shakes his head. "How a beautiful baby girl can shit the way she does is beyond me, though. I swear she smiles when she does it, especially if *I* change her."

I can't wait to be a father. *Fuck,* I can't—I'll get there with her, I just need to keep proving that she can trust her heart with me. "Fatherhood looks good on you." Sighing, I scratch the back of my head. "I wish this was more of a social visit, but do you have the info?"

He grabs a manila folder from inside the car and then hands it to me. "Are you sure this is a good idea?"

When I decided to go track down Shayla's ex, it was more just to watch him and see what he was up to, but the more I thought about it, the more I wanted to send a message. I wanted him to know that I was done fucking around and I was done letting him put that look on Shayla's face that I hate seeing: her brows furrowed, lines around her mouth.

Reece hunted him down for me, so I know where to find him. He's living in Waukegan, which is only about an hour away, so he's close enough to be a pain in our asses. I'm worried he's going to want to try and see Grant. I think it would kill Shayla if she had to share her son with the man who beat her.

"He needs to know that he can't fuck with us—that he can't fuck with *her*. Technically we don't have any proof to show a judge and get an order of protection, and she didn't get one before since he's left her alone until now."

"Whatever you do, be careful. You know I have your back if you need help hiding the body or bail money."

I give him a chin lift. "Thanks."

He takes off, and I climb into my Explorer and make the drive to Waukegan. I plug in his address and eventually reach a brick apartment building that looks like it could use a total makeover. The grass is overgrown and covered in weeds. The sidewalk is uneven, the cement cracked, and the door to get inside is wide open. Obviously they don't care if someone just walks right in.

The interior smells like a stale ashtray, and the carpet feels slightly sticky against my boots. *What the fuck is that brown spot?* I reach Ryan's door and pound until I hear shuffling around.

"What the fuck?" he says. It's almost comical the way his eyes widen, and he tries to slam the door shut on me. Too bad I'm half a foot taller than him, and have a hell of a lot more muscle than him, too. "Get the fuck out of here," Ryan snaps. Too bad I'm not listening to this piece of shit.

After shoving my way in, I quickly scan the space. There's a futon against the far wall, a TV, and a game console. On the kitchen counter are pizza boxes and empty beer boxes. "Nice place."

"Fuck you. I had a nice place until that bitch ruined my life." I grab him by the throat, slamming him into the wall. His face turns red, and he struggles for a breath.

I lean in close. "I want to know what your plan is. Tell me what you're trying to do to Shayla."

Even though his face is reddish-purple, he still manages to smirk at me. "Fuck you!" He tries to spit on me, but I flip him so he's facing the wall, slamming him extra hard because I fucking hate this guy.

"Fuck me? No, it's going to be a fuck you if you go near my family again." They *are* my family, and this guy has no fucking claim to them.

This guy starts laughing—he's nuts. "I had her first. I broke her in for you."

Anger pours off me in waves as I think about the way he probably "broke" her in. I should've brought backup, because I want nothing more than to put my fist through his face. "Shut the fuck up." I'm done with this fucking prick. I can't take it anymore. Leaning in close, I say, "If you don't stay away from her, I will make you wish you were never born, and they'll *never* find your fucking body."

I don't wait for him to respond—I just turn around and walk out.

***

We pull into my parents' driveway and I throw it into park. Deciding for all of us to spend the weekend here was an easy decision. Gretchen and

Grant can hang out together, but we'll still be around just in case. It's been three days since I paid Ryan a visit, and I'm feeling good about my decision to go tell him the what's what.

Tonight we're just going to hang out, and tomorrow Shayla, my mom, and my sister are going for a ladies' day, whatever the hell that means. Then we're going out for dinner while Gretchen babysits Grant.

Gretchen comes out in the craziest get-up: flannel pants, some of those UGGs, the hoodie I sent her when I was in the Marines. It's so big it almost looks like a dress. I shake my head as she runs toward me, except she's not running toward *me*, but right past me to the back door to get Grant out.

"Uhh...excuse me, *I'm* the one that drove us here." I do my best to sound deeply wounded.

Gretchen turns around. "I'm sorry, big brother." She walks to Shayla and gives her a hug. "Hey, Shayla."

We head inside and after greetings are exchanged, Grant carries his bag up to Gretchen's room and I take our bags into the basement. When I come back up, my mom and Shayla are in the kitchen, peeling potatoes. God, this feels so fucking right. Shayla glows under the attention of my mom, and it makes me happy.

Don't get me wrong, my family isn't *The Brady Bunch*—we fight, and I know through my teens I was a nightmare. I'm sure they were worried I was either going to end up in jail or get some girl pregnant. The Marines straightened me out a lot, and I got to see a lot of cool places while I was overseas.

The kids come downstairs, and my mom calls Grant over. "Do you like chocolate chip cookies?"

He nods. "Yes, they're my favorites."

My mom grabs a plate and brings it over to Grant, peeling back the foil. "Well it's a good thing that I made these especially for you." The kid's eyes widen, and he takes the plate, carrying them to the table.

An hour later, we're all sitting down for dinner. I just filled my plate and am digging in when my phone vibrates in my pocket. I pull it out and see it's Marcus. "Sorry, I have to take this. It's about a case I'm working on." I grab my coat out of the closet and step out onto the front porch. "Hey Marcus, what's up?"

"I just wanted to let you know that I'm in town. I'll keep an eye on Shayla when they're out during the day, and then tomorrow night while you guys are out to eat, I'll keep an eye on the house." A couple of the other guys volunteered to do it too, but the fewer people, the better. Marcus has mastered the art of going unnoticed.

"Thanks, I appreciate you doing this."

"Seriously, it's not a big deal. I love Shayla, and I'll do whatever you need me to do to make sure she's safe."

After telling him I'll text him when the girls leave for their spa day, I walk back inside. Shayla looks at me, and I don't miss the worried look on her face. I lean in close to her. "Everything's okay. Marcus just had some information to give me for a case I'm helping him with. I promise." I kiss her before digging back into my food.

We're all lounging around the living room watching *Guardians of the Galaxy*...well, Shayla is asleep with her head in my lap. Gretchen and Grant are asleep on the floor, and my mom and Tad are lounging in their matching recliners. While I watch the movie, my fingers sift through Shayla's hair.

I feel eyes on me and turn to look at my mom, who has a soft look on her face. "I'm so happy for you," she whispers.

I give her a chin lift before turning back to the movie.

***

Gretchen

Today has been the *best* day ever. First, Mom and Shayla made chocolate chip pancakes that were so yumm-o that I ate one too many, but it was worth the gut ache. After breakfast, I had to load the dishwasher and wipe off the table before I got ready to go with Mom and Shayla for the day.

We went to this little salon in the mall, and while Mom and Shayla talked, I just closed my eyes. It was so relaxing, and they had my toes looking totally cute. They're light purple with white tips now. After that, we walked around the mall, stopping in different stores.

While we were in the shoe store, I was looking at some Toms when I felt eyes on me. I glanced up and looked around, not seeing anyone. I went to look for my mom and Shayla and found them looking at shoes for Grunt.

My friends all tease me because I love spending time with that little boy, and I've told them that if Erik and Shayla get married then he'll be my nephew. Of course that's not the only reason I like spending time with him. He's just so cute, and silly. The Tinkerbell snow globe he got me sits on my nightstand next to my bed.

After we finished at the mall, we came home. The guys were all watching some movie about football when we came in. They weren't going out, so I went up to my room to take a nap.

Now, I'm pulling the frozen pizza Grant and I are having for dinner out of the oven. The grown-ups just left, but not without Erik first going over things I already know: keeping the doors locked, not answering the door for someone I don't know, keeping my phone on me, and remembering where the panic button is for the security system, just in case.

"Grunt, come eat," I holler. He's in the living room watching *Boss Baby* on Netflix.

He comes running into the room. "Pizza? Yummy!"

We finish most of the pizza, and I take him upstairs to wash his face off after we eat. We're heading back downstairs just as the power goes off. I grab Grant's hand and pull my phone out of my back pocket. After turning on the flashlight app, I use it to lead us downstairs. "Don't be scared, okay?"

"Okay." Grant's little hand grips mine tightly.

When we make it downstairs, I go to look out the front window and see that our house is the only one completely dark. The hair on the back of my neck stands up when I hear glass breaking in the kitchen.

Grant's body trembles against mine. I lean down and whisper in his ear, "It's okay, buddy." We walk quietly to the hall closet and get inside. I shut off the flashlight app, hearing footsteps.

After pulling up Erik's phone number, I send him a text.

Gretchen: The power is out, someone's inside the house. Grant and I are hiding in the closet. Please hurry home.

I hit send and stick my phone in my back pocket. Grant hugs my waist, his little body trembling against mine. Bending down, I place my lips against his ear. "Erik will be here soon."

The door to the closet opens and a scream slips from my lips.

"Well, look at what we have here," the man says.

CHAPTER NINETEEN

Shayla

We walk into Steak and Chop, and the smell makes my stomach growl. Of course Erik hears it and starts to laugh. I smack his chest and shake my head. The hostess greets us, and she's blatantly checking out my man. Ugh…I want to scream, but it's no use. He's hot and huge—his hotness oozes off him, and it's just something I'm going to have to live with.

Erik and Tad take our coats to the coat check before rejoining us and following to a nice, intimate table by the large fireplace. Erik pulls my chair out for me, and once we're all seated the hostess hands us our menus. She stands right next to Erik while she tells us the specials.

Nicole smiles at me from across the table and all I can do is shake my head. "Sweetheart, it's been this way since he was a teenager. I've learned to just ignore it." A giggle slips past my lips because she says it right in front of the hostess.

She leaves us in a huff when she realizes that

Erik's not impressed with her flirting. I want to stick my tongue out at her, but I refrain because I'm better than that. Thankfully our waiter is male. Tad and Erik pick a few appetizers and wine for us.

My phone sits on the table next to us, and I want to check it. When we were getting ready to leave earlier, I had Gretchen put her number into my phone. Erik leans into me. "They're fine. She'll call if there is a problem."

He places his arm on the back of my chair, playing with the ends of my hair. While Erik talks to his parents about work, I can tell he's vague about a lot of stuff, but I can't imagine it's easy for his mom to hear about the dangerous stuff that her son may or may not do. Hell, I'm sure there is so much more that *I* don't know about.

Our waiter brings out the stuffed mushrooms and bruschetta, and then takes our orders. I'm just taking a bite of a mushroom when my phone buzzes. My stomach dips because it's an unknown number, and there's a picture. Dread fills me as I pick it up and open the message. I bend over and vomit right on the floor.

Erik takes my phone from me while Nicole pulls me into her arms as I begin to cry. There's commotion all around us, but all I can do is squeeze my eyes shut and pray this is a bad dream—that my ex-husband just didn't send me a picture of my son and Gretchen tied up and gagged.

Before I know what's happening, I'm being loaded into the car and we're on the move. When we reach the house, the police are there along with an ambulance, and that's when I see Marcus sitting in the back holding something to his head. "What's Marcus doing here?" My voice sounds detached.

"I asked him to come keep an eye on things while we were gone. It was to give you peace of mind." As soon as Erik throws the car into park, we're all rushing out of the car.

The police ask for a picture, and Erik hands me my phone. I pull up the most recent picture and send it to the officer. I look around for Erik and see that he's consoling his mother right now while talking to someone on his phone.

My phone vibrates in my hand. I've got a text from Ryan.

Ryan: All I want is you. Come to me and I'll send the kids on their way safe and sound.

There's no question I'll sacrifice myself for them. I start moving toward Erik's Explorer, hoping he left the keys in it. I head behind the ambulance and starting tapping out my response.

Shayla: I'm on my way. What's the address?

I hop in Erik's Explorer, crying in relief when I see his keys in the ignition. I turn it on, and as soon as it starts the lights turn on, gaining Erik's attention. "Shayla, what are you *doing*?"

"I'm going to fix this," I mouth. His mom stops him from coming to me. Her eyes are red-rimmed and puffy. She shoots me a dirty look I don't have time to think about as I pull out of the driveway.

When I'm a couple of blocks away, I pull over to

plug in the address in my GPS, but when I start inputting the address, it pops up in the history. "What?" I hit the Go button and head toward the kids.

My phone vibrates over and over but I ignore it; I need to stay focused. My main goal is to get there and have him let the kids go. He's a wife beater, but I hope he wouldn't be stupid enough to hurt a child, especially his own.

I pull up in front of a sketchy apartment building. There are two guys sitting out front smoking cigarettes. I look around the inside of the Explorer for something I could protect myself with. I try to open the glove box, but it's locked—locked could mean weapon. I pull on it until I can get my fingers in there, and then I yank.

It pops open, and all I find is a six-inch blade. That'll work for now. I stick it in my bra. I hop out and lock the door behind me. My hands tremble as I make my way up the snow-covered sidewalk. I slip twice, but luckily keep my footing.

"Hey darlin', how much do you charge? I could go for a blowjob." I ignore the man and walk inside the building. The smell makes my nose burn. I honestly can't believe he's living in a dump like this. We were never rich, but we were comfortable and had a cute little home.

I reach his door and knock. A moment later he opens it and I run inside, but as I move toward the kids, I'm stopped by a hand in my hair. I cry out, grabbing his wrist to stop him from pulling it. How could I forget that he could strike as fast as a fucking snake?

"So glad you could join us, baby. Fuck, I've missed you." He sticks his nose against my neck, smelling me. Nausea pools in my belly. "You smell so good."

I ignore his comment. Gretchen's hands are tied behind her back, and Grant's are tied in front of him. They both have duct tape over their mouths. I quickly assess them, and neither one appears to be hurt.

"That boyfriend of yours tried to intimidate me, but *no one* is gonna fuck with me!" With a quickness, his hand wraps around my throat, and then we're moving until my back hits the wall. My head hits it with a thud, but I ignore the pain. "Do you know what it was like for me in that hell hole? All because you couldn't just do what you're told."

He backhands me, so fast I can't brace for it. I hear both kids cry out. "Guys, I'm okay. I promise." I look at Ryan. "You said if I came you'd let them go. Just let her get our son out of here."

"You're right, I did." He leans in close. His breath is hot and acrid against my skin. I want to gag, but I swallow it down. "I can tell you this, though: Once these brats are gone, you and I are going to leave so we can get reacquainted." Ryan kisses my cheek, and I shudder.

Remembering the self-defense moves that Dalton taught me, I grab the front of Ryan's shirt and bring my knee up, hitting him right in the groin. He doubles over and grips his balls. I punch him in the side of the head and feel excruciating pain shoot up my arm.

While Ryan flops around on the ground, I run

toward the kids, pulling the knife out of my dress. I cut the bindings off both of them. Quickly, I take off the coat that I was thankfully still wearing and help Gretchen slip it on. "The keys to your brother's SUV are in the pocket—go take Grant out there and lock yourself in."

"*Noooo*...come with us, Shayla." Gretchen cries after ripping the duct tape off both her and Grant's lips.

I wrap my hand around the back of her neck. "You keep our boy safe." Leaning forward, I kiss her cheek. "I love you, sweetheart. I love you too, my little Grunt."

"I love you, Shayla." Gretchen grabs Grant, and they go running out of the apartment. I hold up my hands and see that my right one is obviously fractured or at least sprained badly. It's double its normal size.

Ryan reaches out, grabs that hand, and twists. Screaming, I fight the urge to pass out.

***

Erik

Marcus and I pull up outside of Ryan's apartment building and right behind my Explorer. I hated leaving my mom when she was so distraught, but I had to see to it myself that Gretchen and Grant were safe.

I don't know what Shayla was thinking coming here alone. I get out and tuck my gun in the back of my jeans while Marcus does the same. As we head toward the entrance, Gretchen comes tearing out of there with Grant in her arms. "Erik!" They run right into my arms.

"Are you guys okay?" Marcus and I look them over quickly—neither appears to be hurt, and we load them up in the Explorer. "Lock the door, and call the police, okay?"

"D-Don't leave us." She begins to cry. Her body trembles with fear.

I wipe her tears away. "No tears, baby girl. I need you to be brave and look after Grant, okay?" She continues to cry, but nods. The little boy trembles in Gretchen's arms. "Buddy, I need you to be brave. Can you do that? Be brave for just a little while longer." Grant throws his arms around me, hugging me tight. "I'm going to go get your mom. Be brave for me just a little bit longer, please." He nods against my neck. "I love you, son. Okay?"

He looks up at me with those eyes just like his mom's, and nods. I shut the door and then turn to Marcus just as Jack and Reece pull up.

They climb out of Jack's truck. "We thought you could use a hand," Reece says.

Since Marcus got hit in the head, I ask him to stay back and guard the kids until the police show up. I don't need him getting hurt worse. Jack heads around back, and Reece and I go through the front.

"God, this place is a shithole," Reece says quietly.

As we get closer to the door, I see that it's partially open, but there's no sound coming from the room. Jack comes in from the back and sees inside the apartment first. He rushes inside with us following behind him and freezes just inside the apartment.

Shayla is half on, half off the futon. Her right arm is grossly swollen and deformed. *"Fuck!"* My feet come unglued and I run to her. "Baby…Baby, wake up. Come on, Shayla—open your eyes." I check her over but don't notice any other injuries.

"I called 911," Jack says from behind me, and that's when I see Ryan in the kitchen with my knife sticking out of his side. From here I can tell he's breathing…unfortunately.

"Thanks, man. I don't want her in here, but I don't want the kids seeing her." Jack nods at me. I look over at Reece and he's got a towel wrapped around the end of the knife sticking out of Ryan. I move to stand up with Shayla in my arms, but suddenly she's fighting me, screaming and crying. Her fucked-up arm hits me, and Shayla cries out before passing right out. Two sets of paramedics come into the apartment. One comes to us, and they have me lay her gently on the gurney.

I let them know that we don't know much about her injuries. When they wheel them both out, I find my sister has Grant on her lap and they're both crying. I don't want to leave Shayla, but I also don't want to leave the kids right now. The plan ends up being that Jack is going to ride with Shayla, Marcus is going to drive Jack's truck, and Reece is going to drive my Explorer. Marcus will get his car later.

Our caravan makes its way toward Vista hospital. I sit in the back seat with Grant in my lap and Gretchen curled up next to me. Our parents are on their way to the hospital, and hopefully they'll get there by the time we're settled.

As soon as we park I grab Grant, who clings to me like a spider monkey. Gretchen stays close to my side as we all make our way inside. Jack comes out to get me when we walk through the doors. I didn't want to bring Grant, but he won't let go of me. I can tell the nurse wants to stop me from walking back there with him, but I'd like to see them try.

We stop outside the room, and there are two police officers standing there. I hand off Grant to Jack, and they disappear down the hall. I tell them what I know.

"Okay, thanks, Mr....?" The taller of the two officers asks.

"Name's Erik." He hands me his card and lets me know they'll be in touch.

It takes about two hours before they finish with Shayla. While they had her completely doped up on pain meds, the on-call orthopedic doctor came and told us she's got a boxer's fracture in her hand and a fracture in her wrist. He splints and wraps it. She'll have to follow up with an orthopedist to make sure the bones set properly, or Shayla will have to have surgery.

They're getting her prescription and paperwork together now, and she's slipping in and out of consciousness wearing the cutest, dopiest grin on her face. A knock on the door has me looking in that direction. "Hey Mom, come on in."

My mom has been quiet since they got to the hospital. She's held onto Gretchen like she's afraid the girl's going to disappear. I can't say I blame her.

Shayla gives her that dopey grin. "Hi!"

I turn to my mom. "Will you stay with her while I go get Grant?"

"Of course, dear." I kiss her cheek and walk out into the waiting room.

***

A half hour ago, I brought Grant in to see Shayla, and she asked to talk to him alone for a moment. When we walked into the room Shayla was alone, but she seemed off. I asked her if she was okay, and she said she was. She asked me to grab her purse out of my Explorer. She needed to fill out a few forms and needed to make sure they got her insurance information for her ortho referral.

Out in the waiting room, Gretchen is asleep and leaning against Tad. My mom looks troubled and won't make eye contact with anyone. Jack, Reece, and Marcus left after I told them to. I promised that I'd call them if need be.

My phone dings, and I see a text from Shayla. She must be ready to go.

Shayla: I've done some thinking, and I think we should go ahead and end this. Because of me and my crazy ex-husband your sister was kidnapped. He could've really hurt her, and I'd never forgive myself. Trust me this is for the best. I do love you, and I'm sorry I was afraid to say it before. Don't bother going into the back, we're already gone. I'm sorry to leave like this, but I think it's the best.

I dial her number and hold it to my ear—it rings twice, and then I get a weird message. "Dammit!" Everyone looks at me.

"What's the matter?" Tad asks.

"Shayla and Grant are gone."

Tad moves Gretchen and then stands up. "What do you mean, they're *gone*?"

I shove my phone at him, and he reads the message. "Do you have any clue where they went?" I shake my head. "Okay well, where do we go from here?"

"Fuck, I don't know. Why would she leave like that?" I flop down on the cold plastic seat, which groans under my weight.

My mom sits down next to me. "I was upset...I-I wasn't thinking clearly. I *swear* I didn't want this to happen."

"What are you talking about? What did you say to her?"

She begins to cry, and I know that whatever she's going to say is *not* going to make me happy.

CHAPTER TWENTY

Shayla

It's been a week since that terrible day, and it's been hard. I'm right-handed, and it's my right hand and wrist that are broken, but luckily I don't have to have surgery. I'm in a cast up to my elbow, and in six weeks I'll have another X-ray to make sure it's healing properly.

At night while Grant sleeps, I allow myself to cry because Erik's mom's words play on a constant loop in my head. I just remember being high as a kite when Nicole came in, sitting on the chair next to the bed.

"I have things I want to say," she began. "What happened tonight was your entire fault. *You* brought that evil man into our lives, and he could've taken our daughter from us. You and your son need to stay away from us." She got up and walked out after that.

After Erik brought Grant and my purse to me, I ordered an Uber and left through the main entrance instead of the ER where everyone was still waiting.

214

Our driver took us to a motel that was right by a Walgreens so I could get my prescription filled and grab some necessities for us.

Grant kept asking, "Where's Erik? Why are we here? I want to go home."

I just kept telling him that we were on an adventure. That night I slept with him snug against my body. I didn't want to take a pain pill, afraid that it'd knock me out and I wouldn't wake up if Grant needed me, but I was already in a great amount of pain. So I sucked it up and took one.

The next day I called Luna and asked if Grant and I could come stay with them. Of course she agreed immediately, and when we got there, I told Luna about everything that happened while Rocco took the kids for a car ride. By the time I was done, I was a sobbing mess. She gave me my pain pills and then made me lie down in the girls' room.

Everyone from work has been calling me, but I've chosen not to answer. I don't want to admit that everything that happened was because of me. A part of me is upset that Erik didn't even try to fight for me—it was like he just gave up. A relationship between us wouldn't work now anyway, because his mom hates me and blames me for it all, and rightfully so.

The detective I spoke to after my orthopedic appointment told me that once Ryan was well enough he'd be transferred back to jail and more than likely would go away for a long time. When I find another job, my first order of business is to have Ryan sign over his rights to Grant. We don't need to be tainted any longer by his venom.

Shaking off the thoughts of this past week, I head downstairs to my apartment. I use my phone's voice-to-text app to make a grocery list. I quickly dust, and after I sweep the floor, I go around removing the cameras. There's no point of having them since there's no longer a threat to me or my son.

Tears burn my eyes as I grab each one and place them on the counter in the kitchen. I'll box them up and ship them to the office.

I need to figure out how to get our clothes, toiletries, and Lucifer from Erik's place. With my good hand, I rub the pain in my chest. There's a knock on the door, and my pulse races as I move toward it, having no clue who it is. When I look through the peephole, I see Erik's mom. She's carrying flowers.

I wish I was the type of person that could be mean, but I'm not. So I take a deep breath and open the door.

"Hi, sweetheart," she says quietly, holding the flowers out to me. "These are for you."

"Thanks. Would you like to come in?" Nicole nods and steps inside. "I don't have anything to drink unless you want water." I lay the flowers on the counter and wait for her to say whatever she has to say.

"When you're a mom, you do whatever you have to do to protect your children. Sometimes we overreact, and we think we're doing the right thing, but very quickly we realize that it wasn't and we have to figure out how to make it right." I turn to look at her and notice her eyes are bright with unshed tears. "I am *so* sorry for what I said to you. You had been through so much, and didn't deserve for me to throw it all in your face." I hand her a tissue.

"Erik's so upset with me right now, and he's so miserable without you and that beautiful little boy of yours. He doesn't give his heart to many people, but the first time I met you, I knew you were special to him. I hate to think my stupidity ruined what you have. Gretchen told me he's trying to give you space, hoping that you just needed a little time."

A tear rolls down my cheek and then drips onto the floor. "I'm sorry too."

She shakes her head. "You have nothing to be sorry for. *I'm* the one who's sorry." Nicole wraps her arms around me and pulls me into a hug. I can't *not* hug her back, especially after her heartfelt words, so I wrap my arms around her and together we cry until the tears are all dried up.

When Nicole finally takes her leave, she asks me to please talk to Erik. I don't give her an answer either way, but I know it's time for us to talk. First thing I do is unblock his number then read through all the text messages from our co-workers.

Delilah: Hey girl, just checking in. I hope you and Grant are doing okay.

Jack: I want you to call me if you need anything, I mean it. Your job is waiting for you when you're ready.

Delilah: Please text me or call me. I want to

know you're okay.

Carrie: Sweetie, please call us, let us know you're okay.

My eyes burn as I read several more texts from some of the guys. It's the last one from Reece that makes the tears start to slide down my cheeks.

Reece: Hey Shayla, I hope you're recovering okay. I know things have been hard for you. I don't make it a habit of sticking my nose in other people's business, but Erik's hurting. He knows why you've pulled away, and he's giving you space, but if you'd let him know that you and Grant are okay that'd be great. He loves you Shayla, and he loves Grant, and it's killing him not to be with you right now.

I was so focused on myself and my pain that I didn't even think about his. Until now I haven't had someone care for me the way he has, and the fact that he cares about my son just as much makes my heart swell.

I send Luna a text.

Shayla: Hey can you keep Grant for a little bit?

The dots immediately begin bouncing.

Luna: Of course, does this mean you're going to get your head out of your butt and go see Erik?

Shayla: Yes.

Luna: Thank God, I was afraid someone was going to call the cops on him.

I laugh, but then freeze…*what?*

Shayla: What do you mean?

My phone rings and it's Luna. "Okay, he didn't want me to tell you, but he stopped by the first day you were here, and we exchanged numbers. He's called a couple of times a day to check in on you and to check on Grant. He's also been camped out in his Explorer right on our street almost every night. We all knew you just needed some time, and we gave it to you."

Tears burn my eyes because I have such a huge support team led by the best man I know. "I know you have. I'm going to him now."

"Good. I like funny, cocky Erik—not down-in-the-dumps Erik."

We hang up, and I get an Uber to take me to Erik's. Even if he's not home, I have keys to his place so I can wait for him. The driver drops me off in front of the building, and the doorman greets me from behind his desk. I take the elevator up to Erik's floor. My heart hammers when I reach his door and knock. I wait a few minutes and there's no answer, so I pull out my keys and open the door.

As I step inside, shutting the door behind me, I see the place is spotless. I don't know what I was expecting—maybe liquor bottles everywhere, dirty clothes, anything that would say he's been hurting too. I slip off my coat and set it on the couch before walking to the bookcase and picking up the picture of Erik, Grant, Gretchen, and me when we went to get our Christmas tree.

Lucifer comes out to greet me, meowing over and over like he's yelling at me for being gone. I reach down and scratch between his ears, and he immediately begins to purr—loudly.

I hear voices and then keys in the door before it swings open. A statuesque blonde walks in, followed by Erik, and my stomach sinks. They both freeze when they see me standing there. Every part of me wants to flee, but somewhere inside of me my mind is telling me not to move.

"Hi," I say lamely, waving at them with my good hand since my casted arm is in a sling.

Erik's face gives away nothing, and sweat starts to dot my brow—partly from nerves, but my hand is starting to ache and I forgot to take meds. I cradle my casted arm to my chest and shift from foot to foot.

After what feels like too dang long, my feet become unstuck and I move toward the couch to pick up my coat and purse. "Ummm…well, it's been a good visit." I realize I need to give him his key back. "Here, let me get your key." My hands tremble as I try to get the key off my key ring.

A hand stops me, and I close my eyes. It's only been a week, and I've missed his touch so much. I didn't take him for the touchy-feely type at first, but he is and I love it. I want to look up at him, but I'm afraid of what I'll see.

"Look at me, baby." His voice is soft, yet rough, and it's a balm to my soul.

I bite my lip and slowly raise my head until I'm looking into his blue eyes. Tears immediately spill from my eyes. His expression softens, and he uses his thumbs to wipe the tears away. "I'm *so* sorry, Erik. I shouldn't have left like that, but I felt so guilty about Gretchen, and the stuff your mom said was so true." His face gets hard, but I shake my head. "No, she came to me today and apologized. I can't stay mad at her—she was distraught over having her daughter kidnapped."

I hear the door shut, and that's when I remember the blonde. "Oh god, you have a date here. I'm so sorry." I step back from him.

He throws his head back and starts laughing. My tears instantly dry up and I want to kick him in the balls. The door opens again, and the blonde reappears with a dark-haired man, a little girl with blonde pigtails in her arms.

"Baby, meet my cousin Heidi and her husband, Zayne. This little munchkin is Lily. Heidi is my cousin on my dad's side of the family."

That's when I realize they look a lot alike. "It's nice to meet you. Sorry about earlier," I say to Heidi.

She gives me a warm smile. "It's no worry at all. I'm so sorry about what happened to you."

"Thank you. Are you guys visiting or do you live here?" I ask.

"We're just visiting. We live in Des Moines, Iowa. I have to make sure this meathead is doing well." Heidi smiles at me. "Which I can see that he is."

Erik wraps his arms around me, careful of my arm. "Why don't you guys give us a bit, and we can meet for dinner later? We'll bring Grant."

"Lily is looking forward to meeting him," Heidi says, and the little girl nods her head, which makes me think Erik has already told them about us.

They say goodbye and take their leave.

Erik turns me in his arms. "When I realized that you blocked me, I wanted to go to you right away. I knew where you went, but everyone told me not to push you. I was giving you space because that was what I thought you needed. I realize I shouldn't have, but I've never had a relationship before, and I don't know what the hell I'm doing. I'm sorry, baby. I love you, and we should've dealt with my mom together."

I wrap my good arm around his waist. "I love you, Erik. I'm sorry I didn't tell you sooner, but I felt it all the way to my soul. I still do."

He cups my face, and then his lips are on mine. It's a slow kiss, which the longer it goes on the deeper it gets. I open my mouth to him, and his tongue dances with mine. My cast bumps his chest, and I wince. Of course that has him pulling back. "Sorry."

"It's okay, it's just a little sore still. I've been trying to get used to doing everything one-handed, which hasn't been easy."

"Are you up for going out tonight with my cousin and her family?" I smile and nod. "Okay, good. Now let's go get our boy and bring him home."

Those words make me cry, and when we go get Grant and bring him back here, I know without a doubt that we're most definitely—finally—home.

EPILOGUE

Erik

Six months later

"Grant, come on buddy, we've got to go," I yell upstairs to my son, and hear his pounding footsteps. When he hits the bottom he shoots me a big smile, which is missing one of his top teeth.

So much has happened over the past six months. Ryan signed over his rights to Grant, and the plan is for me to officially adopt him once me and Shayla get married. But he's my son, no matter what a piece of paper says.

The day he called me "Dad" for the first time, I almost cried. "Dad? Is Mommy going to be surprised?" he asks as he slips his shoes on.

"I hope so, buddy." We're at my parents, and I'm proposing to Shayla tonight. We came under the guise of a family reunion. When I came up with this plan, I had my eye on an engagement ring at a store downtown, but my mom had asked me to meet her for lunch before I bought it.

Every day my mom still tries to make up for what she said to Shayla that night in the hospital, but my girl forgave her immediately. When my mom sat down at the table, she set a box in between us. I had an idea what it was. I'd picked it up and opened it—sure enough, it was the engagement ring that my dad gave my mom.

It's a gold band with a princess-cut diamond surrounded by smaller diamonds. "Your dad told me a long time ago that if you ever got married, he wanted you to give her that ring, that maybe it would become a family tradition."

Now that ring is hidden in my suit jacket that's hanging upstairs, and we're on our way to make sure the party planner has everything set up.

***

I help Shayla out of the passenger seat and kiss her lips. She's wearing a green short-sleeved dress that shows off her curves, cleavage, and legs. "Can we skip the reunion and go home?"

She shakes her head. "Heck no, I'm looking good tonight." Shayla gives me a saucy wink and struts toward the door. I get Grant out, who's dressed in black pants and a light-blue dress shirt, and we head toward the door.

When we get inside, my mom comes to get Grant and they disappear. My palms begin to sweat, but I'm ready to make this girl my wife. She begins to follow my mom, but I grab her arm. "I wanted to talk to you real quick."

She looks me over closely. "Of course. What's

going on?"

"I love you. I never thought I'd ever fall in love with someone, but then I met this mouthy brunette who scared away every woman from our table. She fought it, but when she stopped, something amazing happened. You not only gave me your love, but the love of that beautiful boy of ours." I reach in my pocket and pull out the ring before going down on my knee. "Marry me?"

She covers her mouth with a hand, tears leaking from her eyes. "Yes, I will." I slip the ring on her finger. Standing up, I wrap my arms around her, attacking her lips. In the background I hear clapping, but I just keep kissing my future wife.

***

Shayla's naked body is curled around mine, and she sighs happily. Our party was a blast, and she was surprised when she saw all our team, Luna, Rocco, and the kids along with everyone else that came.

My girl just smiled the whole time. I don't think she's stopped smiling at all. We got a hotel room tonight to celebrate before we head back to my parents' in the morning. I've thoroughly enjoyed fucking my girl hard, listening to her be loud and explosive.

Her hand rubs up and down my chest. "I've got a present for you," she tells me.

"You do? What is it? Anal?" She laughs, and in the dark I can see her shake her head. "Okay, tell me."

"I'm pregnant. I know we talked about waiting and I got my IUD removed, but it just kind of happened, and I hope you're happy." She bites her lip as she stares at me.

I move until I'm between her legs, my mouth hovering over her stomach. Placing a soft kiss where our child is resting makes a tear slip from my eye. "Oh baby, I couldn't be any happier."

I was, though, when seven months later my son Chance David—named after my dad—was born.

***

Shayla

Ten years later

"I can't believe my sister is getting married today." I straighten my husband's tie as he mutters under his breath. "She's too young." I can only shake my head as he keeps grumbling.

"Honey, she's twenty-four. That's a perfect age. They're both done with school. They both have good jobs. You'd be disgruntled even if she was thirty." I fix my lipstick in the mirror. "I hate to see what you're going to be like when Simone starts dating."

Our three-year-old daughter is spoiled rotten by her daddy and her big brothers, and she knows it. She looks just like Erik, and all she needs to do is bat her blue eyes at him, and he does whatever she wants, even wearing a feather boa for their weekly tea party.

Simone's three big brothers are so busy with sports that Erik takes one day a week to spend quality time with his baby girl. It's so hard to believe how big the kids are all getting. Grant is fifteen, Chance is almost ten, and Reece is eight. With three boys I'd planned to be done—I didn't want to make it four because that meant four *boys,* eating us out of house and home, getting in fights, and whatever else boys do.

But Simone was a surprise, and when they said she was a girl, Erik already started plotting for her protection. It's sweet, but over the top.

"I'm the only man my baby girl is ever going to need."

I can only sigh. "Baby, I love you, but you're an idiot. She'll date, and sometimes she'll get her heart broken. We'll just help her heal, and move on. You're not going to keep her from dating. Sorry, babe."

Grant comes walking in with Simone in his arms. My baby boy is already six-feet tall. He's such a good kid, and we're so blessed. Not only is he a good student, but he's also a good athlete as well. Right after we got married, Erik officially adopted Grant.

Grant and Gretchen may be nine years apart, but they're still just as close as they were when Grant was little. He's her "unofficial" man of honor since he isn't eighteen and can't sign the certificate.

"You look great, honey." His tux is a dark gray, and he's wearing a bow tie that matches the color of the bridesmaids' dresses. "Is she ready?"

"Yeah, Grandpa Tad and GiGi are in with her

right now." He sets his sister down, who spins until her dress flutters around her.

"I a pwincess!" she screams. We didn't show her the dress until this morning; otherwise she would've insisted on wearing—wait, I'm sorry—she would've *demanded* she wear it every day. Her blonde hair is up in a bun with a little crown around it. Simone *does* look like a princess, that's for sure.

After the short and sweet ceremony, we head to the reception. Gretchen looked so beautiful and so happy when she said, "I do." Erik denies it, but I heard him sniffle a little bit. I think Gretchen getting married was harder on him than their parents. David is a wonderful guy, though, and treats her like she's the center of his universe.

Toward the end of the reception, Simone is asleep on her grandpa's lap, and the boys are running around in circles. "Come dance with me, wife."

My big, beautiful, amazing husband pulls me into his arms, and we begin to move to the music.

Ten-and-a-half years ago, I was set up on a blind date…who knew that it would lead to the love of my life? He's given my son an amazing father. He's given *me* three more beautiful children, an extended family I love, and a life so full I sometimes pinch myself to make sure it's real. Resting my cheek against his chest while we dance, I close my eyes and smile.

THE END!

Sneak Peek

HARLEY AND JACK

Rogue Security and Investigation Series
Book Three

Coming Fall 2018!

CHAPTER ONE

Harley

Pulling into the driveway of the blue and brick ranch-style home, I smile when I see "Sold" written in red across the For Sale sign. I've never owned anything in my entire life. Shutting my car off, I grab the manila envelope that holds the paperwork and keys and climb out. I'll come back for my stuff in a bit.

When I unlock the door, I step inside and look around. The furniture looks great and exactly what I picked out. I had it all delivered here as soon as I closed on the house. I do a quick walk through and everything is exactly where it should be, which makes me happy. My office is in the back, with an unhindered view of the backyard and all of the flowers growing along the fence.

The desk is cherry wood and cost me some cake, but when I saw it I knew that's where I wanted to create my stories. I've been writing stories for as long as I can remember, and when I published my first two books I didn't expect them to blow up, but they did. It was slow going at first, but I was happy to at least sell one. But then they *exploded*, and my sales have been growing every week.

In no time I was paying off my debt, student loans, and credit cards. When I started looking for houses I wasn't picky, but it had to have an office space that faced something pretty to look at.

I open the sliding glass door and step out onto the back deck, and then down the stairs. I walk around the flower beds, taking pictures of the flowers so someone can tell me what they are. Male voices coming from the backyard next to mine have me turning to see the men attached to them.

One guy has brown hair and a lean-muscled body, and he's holding a little girl in his arms. The other gentleman has a mixture of blond and gray hair, and when he turns so I can see his profile, I swallow. He's got to be the most beautiful man I've ever seen. His face lights up when he grabs the baby's foot, and the little girl squeals at him.

I watch the little girl lunge for the other man and he catches her with practiced ease. What is it with men and babies that makes women cray cray?

"Hi." I jerk and see that I was obviously staring at them. "You okay?" the younger one asks.

"Y-Yes, sorry, I just moved in. I'm Harley." I walk toward the fence and both men meet me there. I hold out my hand.

"I'm Reece, the little cutie is my daughter, Charlotte—Charlie, for short. This is my father-in-law, Jack." Reece shakes my hand, and then Jack looks at me like I've pissed him off somehow. Reluctantly, he takes my hand in his.

It's probably best not to tell him that when he shook my hand, I felt a zing that traveled up my body. He'd run as fast as he could and never look back. The sad unfortunate story of my life.

ACKNOWLEDGMENTS

First of all I want to thank my family. You guys support me without question every day. Jim, you take on a lot of the responsibilities around the house while I'm on a deadline, and you don't ever complain. You're never ending support has meant so much to me.

Angela I don't know how I'll ever be able to thank you for always being encouraging when I'm ready to quit, cheering me on when I'm afraid, and always reading my words and helping make them the best they can be. I'm excited at what our future holds.

Diane, my PA, my right hand. You do so much for me behind the scenes I could never do this without you. I can't wait until we finally meet in person so I can hug you, even though you're not a hugger!!

Sydnee my amazing editor, I LOVE working with you, you know what I'm trying to say sometimes, even when I don't know how to say it right, and help me craft my words into a beautiful story. I think we make a great team and I love working with you.

Lydia, marketing goddess! Thank you for doing my promotional stuff for this and Security Breach. You're always so easy to work with and I have such great success with you.

To my readers, you're the reason why I love what I do, thank you for your never ending support. I love you all!!

Lastly, Crave Publishing for believing in me and my stories!

ABOUT THE AUTHOR

A Midwesterner and self-proclaimed nerd, Evan has been an avid reader most of her life, but five years ago got bit by the writing bug, and it quickly became her addiction, passion and therapy. When the voices in her head give it a rest, she can always be found with her e-reader in her hand. Some of her favorites include, Shayla Black, Jaci Burton, Madeline Sheehan and Jamie Mcguire. Evan finds a lot of her inspiration in music, so if you see her wearing her headphones you know she means business and is in the zone.

During the day Evan works for a large homecare agency and at night she's superwoman. She's a wife to Jim and a mom to Ethan and Evan, a cook, a tutor, a friend and a writer. How does she do it? She'll never tell.

Stay up to date on the latest news.
Be sure to sign up for my newsletter:
https://bit.ly/1RgXn6V

Facebook:
https://www.facebook.com/pages/Evan-Grace/626268640762539

Twitter:
https://twitter.com/Evan76Grace

Website:
http://www.authorevangrace.com/

Goodreads:
https://www.goodreads.com/author/show/7788444.Evan_Grace